LAST
RIGHTS

LAST RIGHTS

Arthur Douglas

St. Martin's Press
New York

Library of Congress Cataloging in Publication Data

Douglas, Arthur.
  Last rights.

  I. Title.
PR6058.A55456L3 1987   823'.914   86-24816
ISBN 0-312-00138-X

First published in Great Britain by Macmillan London Limited.

First U.S. Edition

10 9 8 7 6 5 4 3 2 1

Most of the Animal Rights organisations mentioned in this book exist, but the characters are intended to be wholly fictitious.

The few figures quoted are taken from *Victims of Science* by Richard D. Ryder, or from data furnished by the Home Office (particularly in a speech made on 27 November 1984 by the Home Office Minister responsible for animal experiments, David Mellor MP). These two sources are not always in agreement.

At the time of writing, changes in legislation are in the wind. The outcome remains uncertain.

G.H.

LAST RIGHTS

ONE

Mary Jennings fidgeted in her chair under the scrutiny of the eyes.

It was, she thought, like being interviewed for a job. In a way, it really was a sort of job interview. She knew that the work was worth doing and she had been vaguely aware of an emptiness in her life which cried out for a cause to espouse. But she would never have put herself forward except under pressure from her new boyfriend, who was dedicated to the verge of fanaticism.

She did so much want him to see her as more than a comforting parcel of flesh. She knew that she was beneath him socially, intellectually and educationally. She was not even beautiful, although he said nice things when he remembered. But perhaps if she joined in his enthusiasms, became an indispensable companion, a right-hand girl like Maid Marion or ... or ... In the stress of the moment she could only think of Minnie Mouse.

She glanced across the table, seeking reassurance from the only face she knew, indeed the only face to which she could put a name. It was not a handsome face, being narrow and rather beaky, but it belonged to her man.

Mike Underhill gave her a nod of encouragement. She was doing very well. Respectful but keen. And once she was fully involved, her mouth would be sealed. He would have a girl whom he could enjoy without the eternal fear that she would betray him in a fit of pique or out of sheer stupidity. He glanced sideways.

The lady in tweed with the mottled face and bolster-like bosom took up the running. To Mary she looked ancient, but Mrs Colcarth was only in her

7

forties. She rarely took an active part in the group's operations, but her enthusiasm, money and organising abilities were a mainstay. A moneyed widow, Mrs Colcarth could always be looked to for ideas, transportation or the cost of a solicitor.

'Tell me in your own words,' she said. 'Why do you want to join us?'

Mary Jennings was daunted by the widow's booming voice and superior accent. Being small-breasted herself, she envied the older woman at least a third of her bosom. The thought distracted her.

Failing words of her own, she skimmed back over Mike's outpourings and recalled disjointed phrases. 'I think it's awful,' she said. 'People think that they care about animals, but they don't want to listen when they're told about all the killing and torturing that goes on all the time in laboratories. And for sport. Animals can't protest for themselves, so somebody has to say it for them. If I can help to make the public see what terrible things happen day after day, just so that new drugs can be developed –'

'And cosmetics,' Mike said.

' – and cosmetics, when we already have more than enough of all those things, just to make money in the market-place, I'll feel I've been some good in the world,' she finished breathlessly.

While she spoke, Mary had been guiltily aware that she was wearing make-up. She hoped that nobody would tell her how many dear little rabbits had died to put her lipstick and powder on the market. At the thought, her brown eyes filled with tears.

The others nodded approval, of her sincerity if not of her eloquence.

Mike, as their host and as Mary's sponsor, had tacit approval to chair the proceedings. He nodded across the table to Eric Foulkes.

Years before, as a university student with a strong leftward bias, Mike had been introduced to the heady excitements of hunt sabotage. His fire had abated as he discovered that the enemy was not composed of a degenerate aristocracy but of down-to-earth bourgeois enthusiasts; and that good working-class citizens – who, despite the redistribution of wealth, could not yet afford horses of their own – followed the hunt by car or on foot.

But by that time his own motivation had changed. He had been exposed to indoctrination of a different sort. Devilment, and an abstract allegiance to class warfare, had given way to sincere indignation on behalf of the injured. It had offended his sense of justice to see a social occasion made out of an intent to kill. It was a small step from the disruption of meets to attacks on animal laboratories.

After graduating, he had moved a hundred miles to take up his first post. He would have lost touch with his fellow-activists but for a chance meeting in a restaurant with Mrs Colcarth. Over lunch, they had found a common interest in animal well-being.

Mrs Colcarth had already been in the habit of sharing her views with Eric Foulkes, the masseur to whom she resorted whenever her fibrositis played her up. It needed only the advent of Mike to turn the duo from indignation to action. A local chapter of the Animal Liberation Front was born.

Eric was a round-faced, sandy-haired man of late middle age. His red nose, the result of eternal hay-fever, gave him the look of a rather jolly gnome. He caught Mike's glance and took up the baton. He spread some photographs on Mike's dining-table. 'I'd like you to look at these,' he said.

Mary studied the photographs, some of which were showing their age, and found them disappointing. It

9

takes an inspired photographer to capture pain, especially the pain of an animal which has no skill in registering emotion for the camera. Few of the shots had been taken by a photographer with any pretension to skill. They showed animals. Some of those animals appeared to have lumps. A few showed signs of injury. It was all very well being shown a photograph of a rat and being told that the rat had been given cancer. Others showed animals which had been cut open, but it would have been impossible for a layman to tell whether the victims had been alive or dead at the time.

Eric's commentary acted as a voice-over, explaining with a certain horrified gusto the abuses which the creatures had undergone. 'Imagine the agony of it,' he said more than once.

'But those photographs give no idea of the scale,' Mike said. 'About four and a half million animals are experimented on each year in British laboratories alone. Four and a half million! Four out of five without any anaesthetic.'

Eric sniffed with more than his usual force. One of his functions was to act as information officer and statistician, and he resented Mike's intrusion into his field. 'Think of apes and monkeys,' he said. 'Man's closest relatives on earth. It's estimated that two hundred thousand die every year in laboratories around the world. That's an average of about one every two minutes, day and night, day in and day out. . . .' His voice droned on. Despite his subject, the effect was soporific.

The steady traffic of sufferers across the massage-couch in Eric's back bedroom was a source of recruits. During the chat which inevitably punctuated his ministration, it was easy for him to probe with gentle hints the attitudes of his patients and, when he found a sympathetic response, to lead on from there. By such a route the Wendocks had arrived.

Hugh Wendock was absent. His wife, Lucy, had been a silent participant but, when Eric Foulkes came to a halt, she spoke up in a soft, shy voice quite in contrast with a bold and brassy exterior. Mrs Wendock had been gifted by nature with the kind of looks towards which prostitutes strive. 'People agree that it's awful,' she said, 'but we're the only ones who do anything positive. There aren't many of us yet, but we're all over the country and we've got the public talking at last.'

'And without hurting anybody,' Mrs Colcarth put in. 'That's important. We give ample warning. We don't even need to do very much. When we announce to the world that we've sabotaged a product because animals were tortured in order to justify its existence, they have to withdraw it from the shelves and examine it item by item, which costs a lot of money and penalises them for what they've done, and the resultant publicity draws attention to the plight of their animal victims. There's a sort of poetic justice to it, don't you think?'

Mary nodded dumbly. Normally a bright and articulate girl, this company mesmerised her.

The youngest man present spoke for the first time. Terry Janson was still a student, and students, although making up the bulk of the membership, were essentially transient and so were considered to be a lower category of membership. He was small, with a round face and protruding ears, but his innocent and almost childish appearance was offset by an expression of worldly wisdom. His had been the eyes which had most daunted Mary.

'You wouldn't consider an apprenticeship in hunt sabotage?' he asked.

Mike humphed. 'Kid stuff!' he said.

'It's not so long since you carried a placard.'

'So I was a kid once myself. At least I grew up.'

11

Mrs Colcarth decided to call a halt. The new recruit shouldn't be allowed to see any diversity of views. 'We don't have to argue about this,' she said. 'We know our own policy – we've discussed it to the point of exhaustion often enough. Hunt sabotage may be a highly desirable activity, but it's not for us. It is overt, public and conspicuous. We are different. Our faces shouldn't be associated with Animal Rights activism at all.'

'Why not, for God's sake?' Terry demanded.

'I should have thought the answer was obvious,' Mike said. 'My face has been forgotten, but you will insist on drawing attention to a face which would be better hidden anyway. That wouldn't matter if we only went in for night-time slogan-daubing or breaking up laboratories. But our next caper's going to require some of us to move around in the open without being remembered. So we just can't use you. That's why not. You sound off about helping us, but you've made yourself useless.'

Terry flushed and prepared a sharp reply.

'Well, now,' Mrs Colcarth said briskly, 'it's time for you to make your mind up whether you're for us or against us. And, remember, there's no going back. Do you want to join?'

Mike was smiling at her.

'I'd like to very much,' Mary said in a voice which had gone squeaky with fright. 'Please.'

'Good girl!' Mrs Colcarth boomed. 'You'll have a chance to prove yourself soon. We have another operation planned. You can go along with Michael.'

Mrs Colcarth awoke next morning – late, as was her habit – with a comfortable feeling that progress was being made in the Cause so dear to her heart. The girl, whatever her name was, had been dismissed from the meeting as being as yet unproven and therefore un-worthy for admission to secret conclave, and the group had got down to what Mike referred to as the nitty-gritty – the details of the retribution which was to descend upon their chosen target.

She was further gratified by a message relayed by her elderly maid. (Her servants were always elderly. They made her feel young again, by simple comparison.) The warden of the nearby Wildfowl Park, which she included among her charities, had telephoned, asking her to call.

She set off on foot and cheerfully. Instead of a boring vacuum of a morning, she could look forward to an invigorating walk in such sunshine as the winter could furnish and to dispensing a little patronage in exchange for a modicum of grateful servility and a comfortable reassurance that she was putting her wealth to good use.

It was soon clear that she could expect no forelock-tugging this morning. Indeed, it almost seemed as if she were the one who was expected to grovel. Well, if the warden thought that she would kowtow to him, he could think again.

Mrs Colcarth turned her monumental bosom to-wards him and lifted her chin. 'I can't help any of that, my dear man,' she said. 'I just know that my dear Sam wouldn't hurt your birds. He's as gentle as a lamb.'

'But this isn't the first time he's been caught in one of my cage-traps,' the warden said miserably. 'I don't want to quarrel with you, Mrs Colcarth. You've been a good friend to the Wildfowl Park—'

'And you've done wonders, Mr Morrow,' she said, holding down the volume of her voice to a pacific murmur. Perhaps she could flannel the silly little man into forgetting the whole unfortunate episode. 'If my contributions have been a help, I'm only too pleased. We must all do what we can to help our friends. How

13

many species of geese and ducks do we have now? Sixty-three, is it?'

'It was,' Morrow said. 'Sixty-one now. We've lost the last of the green-winged teal to predators, and also the Bahama pintail. Obvious cat-damage, I'm afraid.'

'That doesn't mean that Sam has done anything wrong.' She nearly called him her good man but stopped herself in time. 'If you insist on baiting your traps with dead chickens, you must expect cats to take an interest. I expect Sam was just curious. After all, your traps were outside the wire.'

Morrow looked down at the huge, black tomcat which glared balefully back at him through the mesh of the trap. Either would cheerfully have drowned the other. The man sighed. 'Of course the traps are outside the perimeter fence,' he said. 'That's the place for them. Once a predator gets inside, it's more likely to go for a live quarry than for dead bait.'

'Well, then. And your outer fence is supposed to be good enough protection. It cost enough.'

'It's proof against foxes and stoats and weasels,' Morrow said. 'Cats get over anything.'

'Sam just wouldn't.'

The warden's hands twitched but he managed to keep them at his sides. 'If I set traps inside the wire and catch him again, do I put him down?'

'Certainly not. It won't happen.'

'But if it does?'

'It won't. But, even if it did, understand this,' Mrs Colcarth said. She was booming again but she no longer cared. 'If you harm one hair of his lovely coat, I'll sue you. And I'll see that your lease is terminated. If such a thing should ever happen, you might consider sending me a bill for such replacements as you thought were necessary as a result. But, in view of all my contributions to your funds, I'd be surprised if you dared. And

14

now, if you'll let Sam out of that horrible trap, I'll take him home.'

'And keep him there, I hope,' Morrow said. 'Mrs Colcarth, couldn't I even persuade you to keep him in at night? After all, it's only a matter of keeping back his meal until evening and then not letting him out again.'

'He is always in at night,' Mrs Colcarth said, in flat defiance of the evidence.

TWO

Jonathan Craythorne was eagerly removing layer after layer of sheer and erotic underwear from a young lady of exquisite proportions but no particular identity. He had just recognised the pattern of the lace as belonging more properly on Christmas wrapping-paper when he realised that his batman was shaking his shoulder.

'Major Craythorne, Sir. Sorry to wake you, but I think it may be important.'

Jonathan tried to grab at the fleeing remnants of his dream but the image of warmth and softness was already out of reach. He rubbed his eyes. 'Wock?' he enquired.

'An inspector from the local police phoned, Sir. He wanted to come and see you. I told him you were still sleeping, Sir, but he was very persistent. I said I'd call back.'

'Did he say what it was about?'

'No, Sir.'

A cup of tea was steaming on the locker beside his bed, a biscuit disintegrating in the saucer. He drank the tea and shuddered. 'Filthy stuff,' he said.

His batman ignored the comment. The major always greeted the day with the same remark. But let there be no tea at his side when he awoke and all hell would be let loose. 'Shall I tell him to come out, Sir?'

Jonathan looked at his watch. 'No, don't do that. I've got to go into the town anyway. Call him back and say I'll drop in on him. Any time to suit him after, say, an hour from now. Is it army business?'

'He said not, Sir.'

'Then you'd better dig me out some respectable mufti. Was Shona good while I was away?'

16

'Good as gold, Sir.' The batman, who adored the major's red setter, would have made the same answer if the bitch had eaten the chaplain during her master's absence.

The army had taught Jonathan how to respond quickly to sudden demands. It was little more than an hour later when he parked his Volvo in a vacant slot behind the police station, entered the building and introduced himself to the sergeant behind the desk. During that time he had managed to shower, shave, attire himself suitably, eat a hearty breakfast, allow Shona out of the car to stretch her long legs and drive into the town.

Inspector Cheyne joined him in the interview room within a few minutes and the two men looked each other over with the penetrating curiosity common to their respective professions. The inspector was a large man with a flat face from the middle of which a blob of a nose protruded. He had an equally flat, Midlands accent and an air of being more than ready for any tricks. The major, while as tall as the other, was slimmer and gave himself a deceptive air of frailty by his careful walk and self-deprecating manner.

'What can you tell us about this business?' the inspector asked.

'What business?'

'You must have read the papers. Or heard the radio.'

'Actually, no,' Craythorne said. 'I haven't. I've been on an exercise for the last two days and I only got in at six this morning. The only papers I've seen have been maps, and the only radio around was telling me to go rushing over a lot of very steep hills.'

The inspector looked at him hard. 'If you only got in at six, you can't have had time for more than three or four hours' sleep.'

'I haven't.'

17

At first glance, the inspector had put the major down as the soft product of an effete society, but he began to wonder. The major might hide behind a soft manner but, when most men would have shown signs of exhaustion, there was still a spring in his step and firmness in his eye. 'You know a lady,' he began. He paused to examine the other again before looking down at his notes.

Craythorne waited, eyebrows raised. He knew a lot of ladies, but even if one of them was dissatisfied it was hardly likely to be a matter for the police.

The inspector found his place and refreshed his memory. 'Mrs Angela Broderick,' he finished. He turned to a fresh page and picked up a pen.

Craythorne relaxed. 'My sister,' he said.

'I'm sorry,' the inspector said. 'We didn't know that. The neighbour who pointed us in your direction thought you were the boyfriend.'

'There isn't one,' Craythorne said sharply. 'My sister could have told you that. Inspector, what's happened?'

'All in good time. Tell me about the last time you saw her.'

Craythorne curbed his impatience. 'Three days ago. The tenth. I called in to see her. One of my nieces was down with some typical childhood complaint and my sister was rushed off her feet, so I did some shopping for her. I stayed to have tea and looked after the other girl to give my sister a rest. That was all.'

'Tell me about the shopping.'

'Just groceries and some odds and ends from the chemist.'

'What odds and ends?'

'I couldn't tell you. I just handed over her list and got a paper bag in exchange. Medicines for the child, I supposed.'

'Think carefully—'

'No,' Craythorne said, so abruptly that the inspector's eyebrows shot up. 'I've been very patient, but there's a reasonable limit and you've gone past it. I want to know what's happened.'

Inspector Cheyne hesitated. Statements made in ignorance were usually more dependable than those made with the aid of hindsight. But he caught the other's eye and capitulated. 'On the tenth,' he said, 'the Animal Liberation Front sent a warning to the newspapers, radio stations and to us. A ... a certain product had been removed from the shelves of chemists' shops, here and in London. It had been tampered with and replaced, as a protest because the product had been tested on animals during its development. As it turns out, only a small number of items were interfered with, but it's been necessary for every—'

'Never mind all that,' Craythorne snapped. 'Is my niece all right?'

'Your niece was never in danger.' The inspector wondered how to break the news gently and then decided that the major could take it. 'The product was a contact-lens solution.'

'Angela? My sister?' Muscles knotted for a second in the major's jaw. Otherwise, he seemed unmoved. 'How bad is it?'

Cheyne thought that the major must be a cold fish. He had seen stronger-looking men fold up at similar news. 'It's not good,' he said. 'She's in deep shock. Something corrosive was used. Her eyes are badly damaged. They hope that later, with surgery, they may be able to repair some of the damage.'

There was silence while somebody went whistling along the corridor. The inspector added to his notes while he waited for the facts to sink in.

'The children,' Craythorne said at last. 'Who's looking after them?'

19

'We left a w.p.c. in charge until your brother-in-law could fly back from Brussels. I understand that his sister arrived here from Bristol last night to take over from him. Now, perhaps I could have some more facts.'

'Yes, of course.'

'The warning seems to have been given simultaneously with the placing of the doctored bottles on the shelves. Indeed, because of the time taken to go from shop to shop, it may even have anticipated some of the visits. Very few were sold, and none of the others was for immediate use. Also, the purchasers were known to the chemists. Your sister was doubly unfortunate.'

Craythorne nodded. 'She said that she'd run out.'

'And there was no prescription among your purchases. The chemist didn't know you from Adam. But the point, Major, is this. The chemist is sure that he had only just restocked his shelves before you came in. So you may very well have seen the culprit. Who do you remember?'

'Ah.' Craythorne cast his mind back. He had been concerned, that afternoon, with his niece's health and with the forthcoming exercise and had paid no particular attention to his fellow-shoppers. But he had a good memory and a well-trained mind, and his service undercover in Belfast had taught him to keep a mental file of faces. 'There was a fat woman before me at the counter,' he said. 'A lady with a push-chair came in on my heels. And a couple of teenagers were trying on sunglasses.'

'We've interviewed all those. The chemist knew them.'

'That was all, except . . . As I arrived at the shop door, a young man came out.'

'Can you describe him?' The inspector's voice was habitually calm but a sudden rigidity betrayed his excitement.

20

'Black hair, not quite shoulder-length. Thin, diamond-shaped face with prominent cheekbones and a slightly hooked nose. Flat ears. Long upper lip and a thin-lipped mouth.'

'That's very good,' the inspector said, scribbling. 'Go on.'

'Less than my height by about four inches. That'd make him five-nine, give or take an inch. But that included thick, crêpe-soled brothel-creepers. Jeans and a duffel-coat. And he was carrying something.'

'What?'

'Give me a moment. Yes,' Craythorne said suddenly. 'A plastic carrier-bag. It looked almost empty. White with black-and-blue printing.'

Cheyne hid his satisfaction. The description tallied, but was much more detailed and precise than those of the other witnesses. 'You can't remember the shop's name?' he asked.

'Have a heart, Inspector!'

'No, I suppose not. But keep an eye on the carrier-bags you pass in the street, and if you see one that looks similar, read the name and let us know.'

'I'll do that,' Jonathan said. 'One other thing. I have the impression that a young woman was waiting near the shop. I didn't notice her particularly and I couldn't give you even the vaguest description, but she had a carrier-bag which could, no more than could I'm afraid, have been the same.'

'Thank you,' Cheyne said. He finished writing. 'And now, if you'll come with me, we'll see if you're as good with a Photo-fit as you are with a description.'

Craythorne sat where he was. 'Who are these people, Inspector?'

'If we knew that, we'd have them inside. This isn't the first such dangerous caper.'

'No, of course not.' Jonathan could remember other

21

and similar incidents, potentially more dangerous, although in those cases the warning had averted tragedy. 'But if you don't know identities, you must have a general picture.'

The inspector sat down again. He owed his best witness a few minutes of his time. 'They don't keep minutes or hold an AGM,' he said, 'and the membership probably changes from week to week, but they go under the general banner of the Animal Liberation Front.'

Craythorne frowned. 'When somebody calls themselves a front, they mean to imply that they're only the spearhead of a massive movement. And they don't have to make any such implication if there's any truth in it. Everyone would know.'

'That's right. They're not as numerous as they like to make out. But there are all sorts of offshoots and some of the same faces seem to turn up again and again. Animal Rights groups, Hunt Saboteurs, the Hunt Retribution Squad, you name it. They spring up here and there. Some of them are sincere and almost law-abiding. Others are extremist. Many are probably well-meaning, but some are damned dangerous. That seems to be the sort we have around here just now.'

'You have your work cut out,' Craythorne said. 'But the Hunt Saboteurs must surface now and again.'

'And when one of them goes outside the law we have him – or her – inside. And they don't know a damn thing,' the inspector said bitterly, 'or so they say, and the Civil Rights people scream bloody murder until we turn them loose. As you said, we've got our work cut out. But if you can give us a recognisable picture, we'll see if he turns up at any of the hunts.'

'Then I won't keep you talking,' Craythorne said. 'Lead me to your kit of parts and we'll see if I can emulate God and create a human being. With a bit of luck I might even improve on some of his creations.'

Some time later, after fashioning the best likeness he could manage out of the 'kit of parts', he drove away from the police station. Usually, he took pleasure in threading the streets of the dirty, friendly old city, but today he saw none of its mellowed buildings, nor even noticed the sparkle of sunshine on the river as he crossed its picturesque breadth. Outwardly calm, he was seething inside and there was an unusual tremor in his hands. He sucked one of the peppermints which formed part of his drill for stopping smoking, but it lacked the sedative effect of tobacco.

He pulled into the carpark of a pub. He was too careful of his fitness to drink more than the occasional, social pint. But he needed a stiff brandy before going on to the hospital and then to his sister's home. When he came out of the pub, he let Shona out of the back of the car and took her into the front for companionship. Sensing that something was far wrong, the bitch nosed his hand whenever he dropped it to the gear-lever.

THREE

Those who were used to seeing Major Jonathan Craythorne going crisply – and even courageously – about whatever duties the army demanded of him (or, in his other guise as a 'deb's delight', squiring the daughters of his mother's friends) would never have supposed that he was prone to severe and anxious scrutiny of his own motivations.

But so it was. As a child, he had felt the eye of God following him around. In his teens, he had decided that the dogmas of organised religion failed when pitted against elementary logic. During his early twenties he had further decided that certain ancient sins were now both forgivable and fun. But, even so, the ethos of his upbringing stayed with him. Perhaps this was why he and the army suited each other so well. Before joining, he had examined his conscience with care and had decided that the defence of his country and the suppression of terrorism were worthy causes. Thereafter, his duties were clear and there was no more need for doubt.

The appalling damage to his favourite sister, for which he felt no blame but a personal responsibility, revived the old anguish.

Inspector Cheyne's hands were tied by manpower shortage and by the national subconscious prejudice in favour of any animal cause. So be it. The army was not concerned with prejudices other than its own and had an excess of manpower if the user had the means and skill to harness it.

Jonathan was adept at manipulating the military machine. But should he do it? Old ghosts arose, hurling doubts like javelins. Had he the right to take up arms against his sister's . . . what? Attackers? Hardly that. They had not meant to attack. It had been damnable luck that he had bought the stuff, and that she had used it, all before the warnings had taken effect.

What did that make them? Dangerous extremists? Rash fools? Or sincere crusaders on the side of righteousness? No two people would give him quite the same answer. He must decide for himself.

The only animal research facility of which he knew belonged to Gillespie and Baker, the makers of the adulterated contact-lens solution. Directory Enquiries furnished their address, and it happened that an assignment to witness the test-firing of a new anti-tank rocket would take him in that direction. He phoned for an appointment.

The rocket-test, which in Jonathan's opinion proved to be a non-event, was over by midday. An hour homeward on the motorway brought Jonathan to Gillespie and Baker.

The factory was on the very edge of its town. The closure of a coachworks had decimated employment in the area and the local authority, refusing to sit on its hands and weep, had designated a tract of parkland as an industrial campus for high-technology industry and had then strained every sinew to fill it, discarding in the process most of its own and all of the government's red tape. Results had been so good that houses instead of jobs were now in short supply.

Jonathan found Gillespie and Baker in a large, modern building, remote from its neighbours among lawns and trees, with the carparks and loading bays screened by a mixture of trees and creeper-covered netting. The landscaping shaded gently into the original countryside. Jonathan found himself wishing that the average barracks could look as pleasant and as well-kept.

He was taken straight to the room of the General Manager, a pot-bellied man in an unflattering pinstripe suit, who greeted Jonathan without any great enthusiasm.

'We don't usually welcome visitors from outside the business, Major,' he said, 'for obvious reasons. But in this instance, because of your personal and family involvement, we're making an exception.'

'Jolly good of you,' Jonathan said. The fact that he was in uniform prevented him from using his silly-ass act to full effect, but he was doing his best.

The other nodded agreement. 'Not that we accept any responsibility,' he said. 'The product was safe when it left our hands. But we feel we owe you a guided tour. Our Director of Research will be down in a minute, to show you around.'

'Do I get to see whatever it is these people are against?' Jonathan asked.

'Frankly, I doubt if you'll see anything they aren't against. They seem to think that we can do all our testing *in vitro* – on living cells in test-tubes. But how do we test eye-drops in a test-tube?'

'I don't know,' Jonathan said.

'We can't, of course. We try them on animals, just to make sure that there aren't any adverse effects. What's so wrong with that?'

'But how reliable is testing on animals?' Jonathan asked.

The other man had seemed poised with another rhetorical question, but he stopped dead and then resumed in a manner that was both subdued and reserved. 'You'll have to ask Dr Whelks about that,' he said. 'When new drugs are developed we need to know the effect on heart and lungs and kidneys and so on. And especially on the pregnant female and the unborn foetus. The public has a right to it and the law requires it. All right, so animal tissues don't always respond in an identical way to the human, but for the moment they're the best we've got.'

Jonathan decided that it was time to probe for a less stereotyped response, by use of loaded questions. 'Aren't there already enough drugs in the world?' he asked.

'Not by a mile,' the General Manager said. He began to count on his fingers. 'One, there are still many conditions we can't cure or prevent. Two, many people react adversely to the existing drugs for their condition. Three, many of the existing drugs have a risk of side-effects which is accepted but which shouldn't be acceptable. Next time you're ill, ask your doctor whether what he prescribes is ideal, or is merely the best we've been able to give him so far.'

'That sounds very well,' Jonathan said. 'Jolly altruistic and all that. But surely your real motive is commercial?'

'Of course it is,' the General Manager said irritably. 'Whose isn't? Would you do your job if you weren't paid for it? We do a good turn for the government, who don't spend half enough on medical research. But our first duty's to our shareholders. And you needn't look at me po-faced, as if I'd said a dirty word. The shareholders own the business. And the days of the pluted bloatocrat, as one of our union chiefs called them, are long gone. Most of our shares are held by pension funds and insurance companies, so anybody who's in a pension scheme or has an endowment policy is probably a shareholder.' He stopped and gave a harsh bark of laughter. 'I pointed that out to the union the other day. They didn't like it. But we got on better once the message had sunk in.'

'I saw right through the place,' Jonathan said later. 'The Director of Research took me round. Name of Whelks, which sounds a bit plebeian, but he's one of those brainy

27

chaps who look as if they'd jump through the roof if you said "Boo!"'

'What did you see?' Angela asked.

Jonathan looked anxiously at his sister. They were in the living-room of her home, usually spick and span but now showing signs of its mistress's disability. She had been released from hospital, pending surgery on her eyes.

Angela had been a pretty child. As a woman, she had failed to achieve beauty but, when she presented herself well, men remembered her dark hair and oval face as having been beautiful. She was not presenting herself well now. Her make-up was badly applied and Jonathan thought that something indefinable was wrong with her hair. His eyes were drawn back to the haze clouding those other eyes which he remembered as bright with a special joy in living. In the isolation of her blindness, she was glad of his voice; but he was not sure whether the talk should come so close to the source of her woes.

'Of course, I didn't exactly understand any of it,' he said modestly.

His sister laughed aloud, a cheering sound. 'Come off it,' she said. 'You don't fool me with your air of being an amiable idiot. I grew up with you, remember? What did you think about it all?'

He capitulated. 'I saw cages and cages of animals. Rats and mice mostly, but some others. Rabbits, too, and a few monkeys. They were all very well looked after. Some of them looked a bit sorry for themselves and some had lumps or sores. Whelks explained what was being researched, and I couldn't have denied that it sounded necessary. It was unpleasant, though. Most of the animals were having one thing or another tested on them. Later, they'd be put down – painlessly, he showed me how – and all their little bits and pieces examined.'

'And that stuck in your gullet?'

'It did, rather, even when I remembered that those animals had been bred for the purpose. Without the research, they'd never have existed. You could say that they owed their lives to the research, just as we could owe our lives to them. But . . . I can't get rid of a mental picture of being taken into some such impersonal place with nobody to care whether I lived or died. It's a jumble, isn't it?'

'How about the dear little pussies and doggies that people get so uptight about?'

'There were some cats. I only saw one small mongrel dog. I'm told that he's really white, but he was all the colours of the rainbow when I saw him and he seemed rather pleased to show himself off. Somebody'd been doing some research into the fastness of hair-dyes.'

'It's the cosmetic side that really upsets people, isn't it?'

'That didn't seem too bad. And Whelks says that cosmetics only account for half of one per cent of tests. Obviously if you're bringing out a new cream you try it on an animal before you put it on your face. They're working on a new make-up for covering scars. If they're going to test its effect on scar-tissue, I suppose they've got to make scar-tissue to test it on.'

'That seems logical,' Angela said. She wished that she could see his face. 'But you're still uncertain? Why do you care?'

'Because the copper in charge doesn't see much hope of getting anywhere. I might take a hand. What do you yourself think? You're the one who suffered.'

'Leave me out of it,' she said. 'You've got to sort this one out for yourself.'

'I suppose so. The devil of it is that I think they were both holding something back. Not quite hiding any-thing, but I think there was something Whelks would have liked to tell me.'

'They've got to have some secrets,' Angela said lightly. 'Fancy a cup of tea?'

'Very much. Shall I make it?'

'You sit still. I've got to learn to manage. It may be months before they find a donor for me. I get by all right. I can see light and dark and make out vague shapes. The girls are very good.' There was a slight quaver in her voice.

She went out, leaving Jonathan to curse himself for a clumsy idiot. She came back, gently pushing the tea-trolley. 'I couldn't trust myself with a tray yet,' she said. 'Give me time.'

'You won't need long,' he said.

'I'll let you pour. I can do it, but it's hard on the furniture. And take a biscuit. I'm sorry I can't offer you a peppermint, but would it drive you mad if I smoked a cigarette?'

'Probably,' he said. 'But go ahead anyway.'

'Thanks.' She fumbled in her bag for a cigarette, identified the tipped end by touch and found the flame of her lighter by trial and error. 'I daren't smoke when I'm alone. Have you made up your mind yet?'

He put her cup in front of her. 'I don't know how to judge,' he said. 'How do you measure pain, or compare the value of human well-being with that of animals? Whelks is sure he's right, the Animal Rights people are sure he's wrong. What standards can one use to judge? I have a gut-feeling that these people have something valid to say. But did they have the right to gamble with your eyesight for their principles?'

'I don't want to influence you,' she said. She tried to look at him but missed and her serious gaze passed somewhere over his right shoulder. 'At least, I don't think I do. Sometimes I think it'd be satisfying if I had one of them in here and could take a swipe at him with one of Harry's golf clubs. But I'm not really interested in being avenged. Revenge only means that two people have suffered instead of one.

'But there's one thing you ought to know. The surgeon who's going to do my op. was talking to me about it. From what he said, the operation was made possible only after it had been researched on animals. Is that what you wanted to hear?'

'Not exactly,' Jonathan said. 'I think it was what I wanted not to hear. But it'll have to do.'

'Just remember,' she said, 'that I wouldn't want you to do anything . . . drastic.'

'I'm not the drastic type. It's becoming a funny old world,' he said reflectively. 'I can understand lawlessness. I can also understand somebody getting uptight over the fate of an animal. But both of those things in the same person . . .? I thought I was tolerant, but that's beyond comprehension.'

FOUR

Eric Foulkes plied his trade in what had once been a back bedroom in a prim little bungalow. The room still showed its origin in a wallpaper printed with a misty design of roses. Eric had often considered redecoration, but had never found a paper which he liked better, nor the money to buy it with.

Many of his patients were working men, mostly from the local factory of Gillespie and Baker Pharmaceuticals Ltd, whose building dominated the skyline from his window. It was not that firm's policy to give time off for alternative medicine except in the rare instance of industrial injury, so that Eric tended to be busiest in the evenings and at weekends. He compensated for these unsocial hours by maintaining a constant gossip and by keeping a small television set muttering in the corner, to which he could turn his attention if the programme happened to be less boring than the conversation.

Most Sunday afternoon programmes he considered fit only for zombies.

His second patient, a first-time visitor, answered the invariable opening question by saying that he worked for Gillespie and Baker. This made his conversation more interesting to Eric than either his fibrositis or the television.

The patient had good skin and a well-muscled pair of shoulders. Eric set to work under the heat-lamp with genuine pleasure while he led the conversation by stages around to the scandal of animal experiments.

'I don't know anything about that,' the patient said uncomfortably. He had to twist his head round to speak without being muffled by the blanket which covered the couch, and he seemed to have been preceded by a woman wearing a perfume of remarkable pungency. 'I'm only on the building side.'

'Then you must know the inside of the laboratories,' Eric said.

'Like the back of my hand. Nothing unusual about them. Teak benches. Fume cupboards. Electronic balances. China sinks in most of them – chromic acid goes through stainless steel like a bullet.'

This was far from what Eric wanted to hear. 'And the animal-houses?' he asked.

The patient tried to shrug, but his position and Eric's fingers were against it. 'Like the inside of an up-market pet-shop, but cleaner,' he said. 'They spoil those bloody animals. One thing I've noticed about our firm. If you want air-conditioning for the animals, you'll get it all right. If it's for books or papers or a computer, you may get it. But if it's for people, you can forget it.'

Eric was out of temper. His next patient would be a woman and he disliked working on women. Their soft bodies were repellant and if you dug your thumbs in they squealed and never came back.

The patient flinched. 'Take it easy,' he said.

'Got to break up these concentrations,' Eric said firmly. 'Surely you must have seen things you didn't like?'

'I swear most of the buggers are better looked after than I am,' the patient said through clenched jaws. 'The Home Office inspector comes breathing down our necks, and if he doesn't like what he sees he can shut us down instantly. And it's getting worse. It used to be only the animal-houses, but now he has to see and approve every room into which animals ever get taken.'

Eric gave up. It was the same old whitewash. He concentrated on his work. The patient gritted his teeth. If it didn't hurt, it didn't do you any good, so his old mother had said.

The first patient in the evening was of more interest. Not only because of his ailment, although Eric rather prided himself on his success in the treatment of sciatica, but because, as another employee of Gillespie and Baker, he always expressed agreement with Eric's views and had occasionally supplied evidence in their support.

When the treatment was over, the man sat up cautiously and reached for his jacket. 'I'll say one thing for you,' he said. 'When you do a job, you do it. Fingers like steel, you must have.'

'No point in playing at it,' Eric said complacently.

'I got something else for you.' Instead of money, the man brought out some photographs. 'Risked my job to get these, I did. Same terms?'

Eric studied the photographs under the central light. There were two prints of each shot. All showed the same subject, a rabbit strapped to a board. Tubes and wires ran from its body to some electrical apparatus in the background against an out-of-focus tiled wall. The rabbit's face showed pain and terror. There was a hideous swelling beside one eye.

'What were they doing to it?' Eric asked huskily.

'Now you're getting out of my line,' the man said. 'I heard them say something about the stress induced by overdoses of carcinogens. Can't tell you more than that.'

'How did you get them?'

'That's my little secret. I got friends. Do you want them or don't you?'

Eric took money out of the biscuit-tin where he stored the day's takings. 'Twenty quid, less the cost of your treatment. Right?'

'Right. Thanks. Same time next week?'

Eric wrote it in the book. He put the photographs on top of the chest which he used as a filing cabinet, where he could glance at them whenever he passed that way.

When the man got outside and a few yards up the road, he laughed until he had to lean against a lamp-post. He had never been inside the animal-houses or the laboratories in his life. The rabbit had been a road-traffic victim, already long dead before he took the photographs in his own bathroom. It had suffered from myxomatosis, which accounted both for the swelling and for the blindness which had led to a merciful end under the wheels of his motor-scooter.

FIVE

Avoiding, as far as possible, his sister's sister-in-law, whom he disliked intensely, Jonathan Craythorne did what he could for his sister and her family. He had an equal dislike of visiting the sick, but he went cheerfully to read or to bring little gifts which would help to pass the time of sightlessness. While he had an abstract love for his nieces he found their company hard work, but he made the occasional effort when his duties allowed and treated them to the zoo or other suitably restrained delights.

He might have been prepared to put the origin of his sister's trouble out of his mind, leaving the business of retribution to the police. But his services to the sufferers kept his indignation on the boil. The fact that there was nothing that he could do about it only aggravated his sense of outrage.

He toured the shop-windows in the High Street, searching for yet another gift which would please by sound or touch or smell. He was studying silk nightdresses, to the amusement of the more prurient-minded passers-by, when he became conscious that something had passed him. Something half-familiar which he should have seen and recognised.

He looked at the shoppers around him. As far as he could tell, he had never seen any of them before. Their clothes, even those of the girls, had no message for him. Their plastic carrier-bags . . .

That was it! Somebody had passed him with a particular carrier-bag. He turned away from the shop-window, pushed through the strollers and stepped out into the street, forcing the traffic to swerve around him. A white carrier-bag with blue-and-black printing caught his eye. The colours were not unique, but the balance of the design set little bells jangling in his mind. He set off in pursuit.

He was quite prepared to accost whoever was in possession of the bag, but he was spared potential embarrassment when the youth stopped at the first crossing to await the changing of the traffic-lights. Jonathan caught up and stooped to fiddle with a shoe-lace. 'Microchipshop', said the printing, with an unintelligible logo.

The directories in the nearest phone-box gave him an address in one of the smaller streets on the frontier between the town's commercial centre and the sur-rounding houses. It appeared again in the Yellow Pages under 'Computer systems & eqpt'.

He found coins, phoned the police station and spoke to Inspector Cheyne.

The inspector sounded both pleased and surprised. Witnesses usually stopped assisting the police the minute they were outside the cop-shop doorway. 'You're sure it's the same printing?' he asked.

'Ninety-nine per cent,' Jonathan said. 'It's not just the colours, the whole shape of the design looks right. I can't put it into words, any more than I could say how I know my own face from somebody else's.'

'I hope you're right. I'll pay them a call straight away and let you know if anything comes of it.'

'How very kind,' Jonathan said. His car was in a ground-level park nearby. He covered the distance in his deceptively rapid lope, paid his parking-fee and drove out.

The Microchipshop was one of a row of shops devoted to specialist services, huddled together outside the high-rent-and-no-parking district because they could count on the public beating a path to their doors. Jonathan parked, admiring the severe elegance of a kerb undecorated by yellow lines. He spoke a reassuring word to Shona, shared the last two peppermints in his bag with her and entered the shop.

It was quiet in the temple of the microchip. The assistant, a young man with a look of nervous intelligence, finished the sale of some floppy discs to a boy with spots and turned to the newcomer. Jonathan brushed him off and began a patient study of the massed ranks of hardware. It passed the time interestingly enough while the assistant sold a printer-ribbon, a box of computer paper and a disc-drive lead to a series of customers who looked too young to understand the technology let alone pay its prices. Jonathan sighed and felt old. A new day was indeed dawning. He moved to inspect the video films and games.

Inspector Cheyne arrived as the drawing-power of even the more softly pornographic video-film boxes waned. Jonathan felt the glare which scorched across his back. But, after all, the inspector could hardly order him out of a public shop nor demand that the assistant leave the counter unmanned.

The inspector evidently decided to make the best of it. He drew the assistant to the far end of the counter, all of ten feet away from Jonathan, identified himself in a whisper and produced the Photo-fit portrait. 'We think that this man can help us with our enquiries,' he said. 'When last seen, he was carrying one of your carrier-bags, so he may be a customer. Recognise him?'

The assistant studied the picture. 'There's one chap comes in here occasionally,' he said. 'Manuals and textbooks, mostly. Would that be him?'

'That's what I want to find out,' the inspector said. He looked up from his notebook. 'Who is he?'

After another scrutiny of the synthetic face, the assistant shrugged. 'As far as I remember,' he said, 'he never gave a name and I don't remember what went on the receipts. If we're talking about the same chap, he had a girl with him once who called him "Mike", but—'

The assistant broke off and bit his lip.

'Describe the girl,' the inspector said.

A paunchy little man with a veined face and a bristling moustache had entered the shop and now spoke up. 'What the hell's this?' he demanded.

'Oh, Mr Croll,' the assistant said. He began a stammering explanation.

Mr Croll cut the explanation off in mid-stumble. 'If you want to drop our customers into trouble with the police,' he said, 'you can do it in your own time. And you'll have plenty of that,' he added.

Jonathan expected Cheyne to start using his authority, but the inspector walked quietly out of the shop.

'Now,' Croll said, 'we'll try to get back to doing a little business, if you've no serious objection. Serve the gentleman.'

The assistant turned, white-faced, and raised his eyebrows.

Jonathan had not wasted his time while inspecting the goods on display. He adopted an accent which he had almost forgotten, that of the bored and supercilious public-schoolboy. 'I was thinking of a computer,' he named the most expensive on show, 'double disc-drive, daisy-wheel printer, video unit and a hundred floppy discs.'

Croll's eyes glinted. They were talking four figures. 'Show the gentleman—'

'But,' Jonathan said firmly, 'when somebody refuses to co-operate with the police, I always think that there must be something wrong, don't you? I'd hate to be landed with doubtful goods.'

He walked out of the shop.

Jonathan was saddened but not surprised to see Inspector Cheyne loitering outside a shoe-repairer's shop, three doors along the street. He braced himself to accept reproof with proper meekness. They walked to meet each other.

'You'd no business coming to the shop, Major,' Cheyne said. 'Why did you do it?'

'Put it down to curiosity,' Jonathan said. 'I don't think I did any harm.'

'Except to witness my defeat. I suppose you think I owe you an explanation?'

'Not at all. But I think I owe my dog a walk. There's a park over there. Shall we stroll?'

Cheyne hesitated and then gave a nod. 'Perhaps I need a little time to cool down,' he said.

Jonathan collected Shona from the car. She walked at heel to the gates of the small park and then, at a nod from the major, tore away in circles on the grass, sampling the new freedom and its new scents, before retiring modestly into a clump of rhododendrons.

The two men set off around a circuit of tarmac paths between the bare trees. Most of the flower-beds had been emptied for the winter, but there were some late roses to admire. 'So, who's Croll?' Jonathan asked. 'Or am I asking you to breach confidentiality?'

Inspector Cheyne laughed without amusement. 'There's nothing confidential about Councillor Croll,' he said. 'If you were local, you'd know him. His natural habitat is the limelight. He owns a couple of radio-and-television shops, but I didn't realise that he was into computers. He's an independent council-member on an anti-everything platform.'

'Anti-vivisection?'

'Not that yet, so far as I know. But he's a pillar of Civil Rights and Ban-the-Bomb. In fact, anything anybody wants to do he's against it, and if there's ever a story which can make Authority look stupid – which is

40

easy enough, given the right slant – he'll make a meal of it in the press. But just let somebody leak a story which shows him up as less than perfect and he'll set up an immediate scream about breaches of confidence. Accusations of police brutality are his meat and drink. All good, vote-catching stuff, and if he does a little damage along the way, well, that's Politics,' the inspector finished bitterly.

'I know the type.'

'This type happens to be on the Police Committee.'

'Which makes him difficult to lean on? I was expecting you to throw your weight around.'

'You've got it. You can imagine the fuss he'd make if I got heavy with his staff in pursuit of pro-animal activists. By the time he was finished, I'd be personally torturing cuddly bunnies for kicks. I think that we got all that there was, but I'm not sure. I'll see if one of my men can get cosy with that boy in the shop. Don't hope for too much.'

Jonathan said that he wouldn't.

Shona had returned to the grass and, her energy dissipated and her bladder emptied, was displaying herself at the elegant pace peculiar to red setters and few other breeds. A park-keeper approached. Jonathan had already taken the inspector's measure. He decided to apply a small test.

'Does the keeper know your face?' he asked.

'Shouldn't think so.'

'I'm feeling a bit Bolshie myself after this morning. We'll have a little fun.'

The park-keeper was a youngish man, enjoying his small share of power and glad of a chance to impose it on two dignified men and a pedigree dog. 'Dogs must be kept on a lead,' he said. 'Can't you read? What do you think those notices are, Scotch mist?'

Jonathan looked at him coldly. 'What dog?'

41

'That dog.'

'Never saw it before.'

The keeper looked at him suspiciously. 'I'll have to collect the dog for the pound,' he said.

'You do that.'

Inspector Cheyne held his peace, which was all that Jonathan had wanted to know. He would have aborted his little joke had it not been for the keeper's arrogance. He waited until the man had turned away and then palmed a silver, silent whistle from his pocket.

'Let's walk back to the gate,' he said.

'Right.'

Red setters are not the easiest of dogs to train but, perhaps from an obscure feeling that an ill-disciplined dog would set a bad example to the men, Jonathan had taken Shona's training seriously. His patience had been rewarded.

Obedient to the whistle, which was beyond the range of the human ear, Shona sat until the keeper was almost on her. A long shrill sent her out, with the keeper in hot pursuit, and two quick pips set her circling. When the keeper flagged, Jonathan sat her again. By the time the two men reached the park gates, the keeper was tottering. Shona, entering thoroughly into the game, was enjoying herself. But enough was enough. Jonathan whistled her to come.

The keeper arrived, gasping, as Shona entered her bed in the rear of the estate-car. 'Your dog—'

'What about my dog?' Jonathan asked coldly.

'You said you'd never seen it before.'

'When did I ever say that?' Jonathan slammed down the door. 'I've never seen *you* before, and the dog hasn't been out of the car.'

The keeper turned to Inspector Cheyne. 'You saw him. You heard him. Surely.'

'I've never seen either of you before,' the inspector

said, walking off.

Jonathan settled himself into the car and drove away. So, he decided, the inspector might not be overly concerned with the book of rules once the ice was broken.

SIX

In Eric Foulkes's fussy living-room the senior local members of the Animal Liberation Front were arguing, not for the first time, over the outcome of their venture against the products of Gillespie and Baker. Their host had gone to some trouble with dainty cups and china tea and some fancy biscuits, but the refreshments were almost untouched.

'It was an absolute disaster,' Mrs Colcarth declaimed in a voice which rattled the glass animals on the cocktail cabinet. 'It's ruined our image and alienated public sympathy.'

'It was unfortunate, but it's all publicity of a sort,' Eric said. He spread some press-cuttings on the tiled coffee-table. 'People are paying attention to us, this time.'

'We can do without this sort of attention. We were beginning to gain acceptance as serious people with a sound purpose, but now we're branded in the public mind as irresponsible fanatics who blind young women.'

'Don't get your knickers in a twist,' Mike Underhill said. (Mrs Colcarth's eyebrows shot up.) 'It was just her bad luck. According to the media, the silly bitch had run herself out of the stuff. So her brother fetched it and she put her lenses in straight away, before our warning took effect. He must have been right on my heels. In fact, I think he passed me in the shop door – the papers said that he's an army officer, and I crossed with a man of about the right age who looked to be the sort of unthinking Sloane Ranger type which is all we've got to defend us these days, God help us! Nobody could have foreseen a coincidence like that. The public will realise.

44

Or they'll forget. They're good at forgetting.'

The fourth member present was Hugh, husband of Lucy Wendock. It was her turn to mind the baby. He shared none of his wife's brazen looks, being a bony and colourless young man with badly-chosen spectacles balanced on a nose which was too small to support them. The couple were vegetarians, health-food addicts, nuclear protesters and followers of any other doctrine which can soothe the sort of conscience which aches for other people's sins.

'Do you think he'll remember you?' Hugh asked anxiously.

'Shouldn't think so,' Mike said contemptuously. He despised Hugh, as he despised almost everybody. 'He looked as if he'd have difficulty remembering his way home.'

'All the same, I think we should lie doggo for a while. If one of us gets caught in some other act, it could land us all in a jam. We went outside the law and somebody got injured. That could be serious. She could sue. That wouldn't look good in the papers. And it would cost.'

Mrs Colcarth looked even more thoughtful. She could guess who would be left to foot the bill. 'Hugh's right,' she said. 'We need time for the fuss to die down. Let the silly girl have an operation and get her sight back.'

'That could take months or years or for ever,' Mike said. 'I vote we strike again now. If you've all got cold feet, we could make it something non-toxic. Shampoo with stain in it, which would make people look stupid without hurting them. Then we wouldn't need to give a warning at all and nobody would be watching out for known faces until much too late. Let's have a look at the black-list. There's bound to be something suitable.'

Eric broke an uneasy silence. 'How's your young lady taking it?' he asked. 'It'd be a pity if she turned soft and

45

blurted something out.'

'She nearly wet herself when it happened,' Mike said. 'I pointed out that she was just as guilty as any of us. She saw sense in the end. And she's tougher than you'd think to look at her. She's game for another strike now.'

'Well, I'm not,' Eric said. 'Hugh's right. Anybody getting caught pulling the same sort of stunt again would be in deep trouble and a danger to the rest of us.'

'Not if we changed our line of attack, and claimed the credit under another name,' Mike said.

'Like what?'

'Mink farm?' Mike suggested. 'I've marked one down and studied the layout.'

There was a spurt of argument. Mrs Colcarth trod it down. 'We need to think it over,' she said, 'and to get opinions from the others. And the only mink farm within reach is just a few miles from my house.'

'If you're all too scared,' Mike said, 'I don't mind doing it on my own. It would really hit them where it hurts. Mink play hell with the fishing and shooting, and the loss of his stock hits the fur-farmer where it hurts most – in the pocket. There's a lot of money in mink.'

'You needn't be alone,' Terry said from the window.

'And if you're going to be a one- or a two-man band,' Hugh said bravely, 'we don't want to know you. Let's have a few days to think.'

Eric caught Mike's eye and held it for a moment. 'It needs thinking about,' he said. Terry noted the glance.

The meeting broke up a few minutes later. Mike offered Terry a grudging lift, but Mrs Colcarth stayed behind. Never one to waste a journey, she had booked a session on the masseur's couch.

When she was reduced to a prone carcass in the minimum of pink crêpe de Chine, Eric laid the rabbit photographs on the carpet under her overhanging nose.

46

'Good, aren't they?' he said.

'Terrible.' She looked again. 'Terribly good. Well done! Are they from the same place?'

'Yes.' Eric repeated the bald explanation which had come with the photographs.

'They're too good to keep to ourselves. We'll have to send them to our friends in London. How much did you pay for them?'

'Fifty.'

Mrs Colcarth jumped under the probing fingers. 'That's rather a lot.'

'He risked his job. And look at the use we can make of them.'

'That's true. All right,' she said bravely, because, after all, it was for the Cause and there was so little that a poor, weak woman could do. 'It shall be reimbursed.' She relaxed under the strong fingers and looked again at the photographs on the carpet. Eric, breathing heavily, leaned to look over her shoulder.

'Of course we must go on,' she said. 'Of course we must.'

Mrs Colcarth's brave words found a muted echo in a bright but cheaply-furnished living-room, fifteen miles to the south.

'Of course I care,' Hugh Wendock said without passion. 'I've told you often enough.'

'Telling's all very well,' his wife said. 'Doing something about it's another.'

'I wouldn't mind fund-raising or writing letters or even speaking at meetings. But I can't afford to get caught breaking the law. I've a responsible position to live up to.'

'You're a clerk,' said Mrs Tilson.

Hugh looked at his mother-in-law without affection. It was a bit much, to arrive home from a difficult meeting, with important matters to be discussed, and to find his mother-in-law not only present but determined to join in discussing a subject of which she had limited knowledge and almost no comprehension. He hoped that his wife's coarse good looks would never turn into this travesty of lace and perfume and drooping flesh. The frequent presence of Mrs Tilson about the house was a hell of a price to pay for an occasional baby-sitter who was never available when it really mattered.

'I'm an executive officer,' he said coldly.

She sniffed. 'That's what they call it now, is it? Well, if it's so responsible, why doesn't it pay more? Why's my daughter stuck in a mid-terrace house in a new estate? Tell me that.'

'We're saving,' he said. It was true, by a small margin.

Lucy, thank God, had not inherited her mother's strident voice. 'We can't not go on,' she said. 'A hundred million animals die in laboratories every year, round the world. In this country—'

'I know the figures,' he said gruffly.

'But people don't. They pay no attention except when it's pushed under their noses. All right, it was unlucky about that woman. But it wasn't meant to happen, so it was purely an accident. And they'll fix her up. They can do wonderful things nowadays.'

'But the risk, Lucy,' he said.

'It's a very small risk. Think of all those animals. And most of them die in experiments on cosmetics, not medicines. Think how grateful they'd be.'

The concept of a hundred million rats and guinea-pigs queuing up to shake his hand was beyond him. 'If I got convicted of an offence, it'd mean my job,' he said.

'They took the assistant managing director back when he came out of jail,' Lucy pointed out.

'That was different. He falsified some returns but he

48

did it for the good of the firm.'

Mrs Tilson had been silent long enough. 'If that Mrs Colcarth's in it,' she said firmly, 'it must be all right. She's a lady. She'd see that you didn't suffer.' The shrill virago from the town and the booming dowager from the County had met once or twice. Each recognised her counterpart immediately and, secure in a clear understanding of their roles, they had reached an immediate rapport.

'She's becoming very fond of you,' Lucy said. 'She's very rich and she doesn't seem to have any relatives.'

'There you are, then,' said Mrs Tilson.

Similar thoughts had passed through Hugh's mind occasionally, although he had never dared to speak them aloud. But since it had been mentioned ... 'She'll probably leave the lot to the RSPCA,' he said.

'Not in a million years,' Lucy said. 'She thinks they take too soft a line. And she can't leave it to the ALF because it's not a legal body.'

He shied away from the subject. 'We're sailing too near the wind for my liking,' he said. 'And some of the students think it's all one great prank. It's all going to end in tears, one of these days.'

'You don't have to go out when you think the plan isn't foolproof,' Lucy said. 'In fact, that might be a good line to take – the sensible one who points out any weak bits in the planning. And you could certainly refuse to go along if those students were there. The others would think that was only sensible. I could see that Mrs Colcarth herself doesn't trust them.'

'That's settled, then,' said her mother comfortably. 'Now, Hugh can bring us a nice cup of tea, if you trust him with your china, while we have a little chat.'

When Mrs Tilson at last took her departure, her nearest and dearest shared a sigh of relief. The older woman was inclined to linger. She, after all, did not have to get up by the clock in the morning.

'Tired, darling?' Lucy said, locking the front door. 'Never mind. I'll just take a look in on the baby and then we can get to bed. In one way, it's a pity he wasn't a girl. If we get a girl, we could name her after Mrs C. That should swing it. I wonder what her first name is. Something awful, I expect.'

'We can't afford another child yet. I've told you.'

'Well, when we do. Coming up?'

Hugh had sat down. He got to his feet, yawning. 'I think I'm too tired to sleep,' he said.

She put her arms round his neck and licked his ear. 'We can always do something to help you sleep, can't we?'

Hugh stopped yawning and considered it. He was tired but . . . 'If we do it for me,' he said.

'No, it's my turn.'

Hugh tried not to lose interest. He had never been an enthusiast for an exchange of oral sex. But Lucy stayed firm. As she pointed out, if they couldn't afford another child, hers was the most certain form of contraception. And she never could enjoy it the same in the only way which seemed to turn him on. Loving bondage it might be, but he applied it with a little too much enthusiasm. And Lucy was a girl who liked to feel that she was in control of things.

SEVEN

Major Craythorne stood up to look around the recreation room attached to the NAAFI. About forty men were present and each had a glass of beer in front of him – this was typical of the gestures which had made him that unique animal, a well-liked officer. At his side sat a ruddy-faced, stocky civilian in a suit of rough tweed but good cut.

Craythorne had a knack with voices. His CO had once said, meaning it as a compliment, that Jonathan should have been an actor. Now, he pitched his voice midway between the public-school tones which he used when he wished to be underrated and the crisp, army voice which could have men jumping through burning hoops without asking any questions. He could also pass for Irish, and had done so at risk to his life.

'I don't suppose many of you know or care much about fox-hunting,' he began, 'and there isn't time to discuss it in any detail. But if any of you are on the side of the fox, or if you have sympathy for the Animal Rights activists who've been getting so much publicity lately, you're free to leave now.'

Nobody moved. Looking round the young faces in the room, he thought that his NCOs had chosen well. A good NCO knows far more about the men under him than they would ever have suspected.

'I may as well tell you now that the rest of the unit will be going out on Thursday, to do a forced march of thirty miles in full kit. You're welcome to join them, but I can offer you a rather more interesting day in the country.'

There were smiles and a quickening of interest. He dropped his voice and went on.

'As most of you know, my sister was blinded recently. They hope to save her sight when a donor for corneal grafts turns up, but for the moment she's sightless. And she's the mother of two young children. This happened because fanatics put a bottle back on the shelves in the chemist's shop after doctoring it, in order to get publicity for their attitude to medical tests and experiments using animals. Well, they're entitled to their views. But they're not entitled to blind my sister to make their point. And I was the one who made the purchase and took the stuff home to her, so I feel very much involved. I propose doing something about it. I want to find these people and I want your help.'

He paused to test the atmosphere, like a dog sniffing the wind. So far, they were with him.

'It seems certain that I passed the man who planted the doctored material, and you'll all be given copies of the Photo-fit picture which I made up. The copper in charge of the case has promised to distribute it as widely as he can. We believe that the man is known as Mike. Those are almost the only leads we've got. Extremists like these don't advertise in the Yellow Pages.

'But you would expect links between them and other activists like the Hunt Saboteurs, whose antics are necessarily more public. If they're not the same people, they know each other.

'On Thursday, the Hunt meets at Ansdown Park Hotel. They've been plagued by saboteurs recently. This gentleman on my left, by the way, is the Master. Usually, the Hunt tries to confine the dates and places of its meetings to its own members, to make it more difficult for the saboteurs, but this time the news has been carefully leaked.

'You've been picked because you all look young enough to pass for students.' There was a ripple of amusement. 'Or rough enough to pass for Rent-amob.' Open laughter. He waited for it to die away. 'The Hunt will meet at nine and move off at nine-thirty. It's too much to hope that our man will be there. But you'll be there and you'll mingle with the saboteurs. The University's in recess, so there should be a good turnout. Civvies such as a student might wear, and suitable shoes or boots but not army clogs – any difficulty over clothing, see me later. You'll be equipped with aerosols of Antimate or similar but you do not, repeat not, go so far as to spray it into the faces of hounds. You can pretend to, but don't. Got that?

'We don't want word getting about, so you must all act more or less simultaneously. The Hunt moves off at nine-thirty. By ten, saboteurs' activity is usually over. But between nine-thirty and ten there's a lot of milling around and they tend to split into small groups. You'll do the same and try to attach yourselves to individuals or pairs of saboteurs. At nine-forty-five precisely, you produce one of these pictures, show it to the others and make some comment about it. I leave it to your intelligence what sort of remark you make, but if any of you is too thick to think of one, come and see me.' More laughter. 'I suggest, "Not much of a likeness", or "He'd better keep his head down for a bit". That sort of thing. It's odds-on that some of them know him, and that one of them will let something slip. Every least comment gets reported back to me. Got it?'

Heads nodded, like pecking hens.

'In return for his co-operation, the Master would like a little help from us,' the major resumed. 'I'll let him speak for himself. Mr Stimson.'

The MFH got to his feet. 'This isn't the time for a justification of hunting,' he said, 'although I could speak for hours on the subject. So I'll only' mention that hunting with hounds is the only method of fox-control in which the fox either escapes completely or is killed quickly. A more important point is that, whatever your views, fox-hunting is legal. These saboteurs use illegal methods to disrupt a legal activity which has been part of our tradition for hundreds of years and which is much loved by those who join in.

'So the saboteurs are the law-breakers, but it's difficult for the law to deal with them. The police turn up to keep order, but wherever the police are the action stops. And afterwards it's all, "Please, Officer, it wasn't me who pulled Mr Smith out of his saddle, threw cow-shit at the lady or stung the little girl's pony with an air pistol so that she got thrown on her head." Those are actual, recent examples, by the way.

'The last thing that we want is to meet violence with violence. What we need is the hard evidence of at least two witnesses connecting individuals with each specific incident. Especially incidents of violence or of cruelty to animals, to remove the sympathy which these people so often get from those who take a superficial view of the subject. With photographs if possible. Given that sort of evidence, we can get court orders against the ringleaders.

'I'm not offering any rewards, because evidence which is bought isn't worth having. But the Hunt is making a donation to your Welfare Fund whether or not you do any good, and we'll be happy to pay for any film or other expenses.' The Master paused and then sat down.

'Any questions?' Craythorne asked. He stared at a thick-looking fellow at the back. The major knew that the most useful part of a briefing often came from the questions. He also knew that the men needed a first question to give them time to think. It was his habit to plant a man with a stupid question to set the ball rolling.

The man got reluctantly to his feet. 'I'd like to ask the Master why they have to wear red coats,' he said.

There was a chorus of derision but the Master stood up immediately. 'I'd like to answer the question,' he said. 'It's a subject which, for some obscure reason, often turns out to be emotive. People who honour traditions of dress when attending their own sports resent it bitterly when we do the same.

'The answer to the question lies partly in tradition, but there's a very sound reason behind it. If you're leading the field and you come a cropper over a hedge, it's a great comfort to know that those coming behind can see you on the ground, even through the hedge. A ton of horse is grand to have under you but not much fun when it lands on top.'

The ice was broken. A thin soldier in glasses got up. 'Would the Master please give us more details of what sort of incidents we should be watching for . . . ?'

On the Thursday afternoon, the first trickle of men returned early – those who had nothing to report and who had lost touch with the hounds. Just after dark there was a sudden influx of most of the remainder, chattering like geese about the day and exchanging ribald banter. They settled down and lowered their voices while a fresh-faced corporal, chosen for command in the field solely on the grounds of his youthful appearance, made his report.

'Never saw such a disorganised shower as them saboteurs, Sir. Our lads could ha' done a far better job of breaking up a hunt. The MFH is tickled pink. Four prosecutions pending, well backed up with evidence. One of them's a ringleader who already had a court order restraining him, and Jukes got a Polaroid photograph of him firing a catapult at a horse, so he's for the high jump.'

'Jolly good,' said the major. 'But that was a sideshow. What about the main event?'

55

An eager private had been hovering in the background. The corporal turned and nodded. 'Collins can tell you himself, Sir. It's not much, but it may help.'

Collins snapped to attention, looking faintly ridiculous in his anorak and washed-out jeans. The major smiled. 'At ease,' he said.

'Sir. At nine-fifteen I'm close to one of the girls.' There were subdued cheers from his mates. 'So I whips out—' The cheering rose to cut him off.

'Let him tell it,' the major said. There was an instant silence. The major would stand for high spirits, but never for disobedience.

Collins was pink but determined. 'I gets out the picture and shows it her. "If that's meant to be Mike, it's not very good," I says. "But he'd better keep his head down for a bit," I says. She looks at it and she says "I saw that in the Post Office," she says. "Mary Jennings won't be too pleased," she says, "she thinks the sun rises and sets behind his pecker." That's what she says, Sir, near as I can remember. She'd've said more but her boyfriend shut her up quick. Does it help, Sir?'

'I don't know yet,' Craythorne said. 'But it's the best we've got. Well done, Collins. Are you sure it was Jennings? Not Jenkins?'

'Jennings, Sir.'

'Sir! Sir!' A toothy soldier with oiled hair and brash good looks stepped forward.

'Yes, Evans?'

'I met a Mary Jennings. 'Bout three months ago. Took 'er 'ome from a disco, didn't I?'

The major killed the comments with a quick frown. 'Where was her home?'

'Don't remember the address, Sir, do I? But I could point it out. One of the council houses up the back of the town.'

The major wondered whether Mary Jennings had

56

been the girl in the computer shop or outside the chemist's, or both. 'Describe her,' he said.

'Just a bird. Neither this way nor that. Long hair, sort of brown, that's all I remember, isn't it? She wasn't for any fun so I never saw her again. Got a knee in the goolies when I tried it on, didn't I?'

'Don't blame 'er,' said a voice. 'I'd of done it twice as 'ard.'

No other information had been gleaned. When Jonathan dismissed the men, three remained behind. They wanted to know whether the army would give them passes and other help towards riding lessons.

The major sighed and said that he would look into it. He wondered how he came to land himself with these burdens. His men, who would not have thought to make such a request of any other officer, could have told him.

EIGHT

The weather had turned crisp and bright. They met out of doors in a favourite place, a layby high on a hill. There they could gaze for miles while they talked, and enjoy a benign sense of responsibility for the visible wildlife and for other creatures which would remain shy only until reassured that Man had mended his hostile ways.

Mrs Colcarth's Daimler arrived first. She had collected Eric Foulkes on the way and had taken the offer of a free massage in payment for his fare. She felt both relaxed and stimulated. It would have been more stimulating if Eric had been a macho type, but Mrs Colcarth could fantasise as freely as any other middle-aged widow. Surely he must have lusted after her? Only the finest silk, and pink at that, had separated him from her delicate flesh. And she was not lacking in womanly endowment. It was not every woman of her age who could still drive men mad.

Hugh and Lucy Wendock arrived together. Mum was baby-sitting. They came in a rusty Mini which, parked behind Mrs Colcarth's car, looked like an intrusive urchin at a function.

Mrs Colcarth, still cosy from the heat-lamp, had no intention of facing the cold air. The Wendocks got into the back of the Daimler, settling into its comfort with appreciative little noises. It would be a week before they could reconcile themselves to their humbler transport again.

'Have you seen the local paper?' Lucy asked.

'I left home before it was delivered,' Mrs Colcarth said. 'Living out in the country . . .'

'You'd better take a look,' said Hugh. He passed a

copy forward. Eric and Mrs Colcarth leaned together to read an item which had been ringed in black felt-tip pen.

'RAID ON MINK FARM', said the headline, and 'MAN DEAD'.

'Oh my God!' said Mrs Colcarth.

'It isn't as bad as it looks,' Lucy said. 'First signs are that the man died of a heart attack. You'd better read on.'

They read on. The story was bare of details. 'Ridgeback Fur Farm,' Eric read out. 'Isn't that the place Mike was talking about?'

'Of course it is,' said Mrs Colcarth. 'I can see it from my front windows, across the valley. The only blot on the landscape.'

'That's what I thought,' said Hugh. 'But he'd never have tackled it on his own. Would he? I take it that none of us . . . ?'

'Obviously not,' Eric said.

'But he could have taken his girl with him,' Lucy said. 'Or that student. It says here that a phone-call to the paper claimed responsibility on behalf of the Justice for Animals League. Never heard of them.'

'Nor I. I'm sure that Mike and . . . what's her name? Something common. Mary, that's it. I'm sure they wouldn't act alone.' Mrs Colcarth sounded far from sure. 'Anyway, as long as there's no proven connection it needn't affect our actions.'

'Surely we're not moving again so soon?' Hugh said. 'At the moment, public concern is more with the blinded woman than with the animals. And now a dead man . . .'

'And now's a good time to make them change their point of view,' Mrs Colcarth said briskly. 'Show them the photographs, Eric.'

Eric passed a set of prints back over his shoulder. 'These come from Gillespie and Baker,' he said.

The couple in the back seat looked at them. Lucy gave a faint moan.

'Surely,' said Hugh, 'these will have the same impact in a month's time? Or wouldn't a press release be enough?'

'My dear boy, you know what happens to our press releases. The guilty deny everything. They say that our photographs are old or foreign or faked, or all three, and our sources can't come out into the open to back them up. The public end up not believing us, mostly because they can't believe that men and women like themselves could do such things and on such a scale. The facts go beyond credibility.'

'What have you in mind?' Lucy asked, frowning. She handed the photographs forward again.

Mrs Colcarth looked down at them and gave a ladylike shudder. 'We must go in and get hard evidence,' she said. 'Then the public will believe us. Their indignation will rise and they'll forgive us for the other unfortunate incident.'

'But could we do it?' asked Lucy.

'It's possible,' Eric said thoughtfully. 'I know the layout – I have several of their staff among my patients. There are two men on duty overnight. One is supposed to be on patrol while the other watches closed-circuit monitors in the gate-house. They change over every hour on the hour, but they usually have a mug of soup or something together. I walked in on them at such a time the other night, to ask the way somewhere. I was able to keep them talking for almost half an hour. Nobody was watching the screens and I know that they don't have any automatic alarms. Anybody could have walked in.'

'What I have in mind,' Mrs Colcarth said, 'along with gathering what evidence we can get, is a mass release of animals. Let them see that dogs and cats are used. And a plague of rats should make them sit up and take notice.'

'I don't think laboratory-bred white rats would survive long in the wild,' Hugh said.

'But Joe Public doesn't know that,' his wife pointed out. 'I think Mrs C's right. I hate rats.'

'It's not right to hate any of God's creatures,' Mrs Colcarth said severely. 'I have a fear of rats, but that's only my silliness and I'm trying to overcome it. Here's Mike at last.' She wound down her window. 'Where on earth have you been?'

'Coping with troubles,' Mike snapped back, stooping to lean his elbows on the door. He had had a haircut and seemed to be growing a moustache.

'Hop in and tell us about it,' Lucy said.

'I'm all right here.'

'Well, I'm not,' Mrs Colcarth said. 'I've just been under Eric's heat-lamp and there's a howling gale down my neck.'

Lucy prepared to squeeze up but Mrs Colcarth beat her to it, pushing open the driver's door and moving over so that one broad buttock was on either seat. Eric cringed away from her. Mike and Lucy would both have preferred him to be pressed against Lucy's softness, but the older woman was quite capable of throwing a tantrum if thwarted. He winked at Lucy, squeezed himself behind the wheel and tried to ignore the warmth of a hip which was flabby but restrained, like an overfilled hot-water bottle.

'What troubles?' Hugh asked.

'You've seen the Photo-fit that's been circulating since our caper with the chemists? It's meant to be me, even if it's not very flattering.'

'I wouldn't have known it for you if I hadn't known you were there,' Lucy said.

'Bless you, my dear, you comfort me,' Mike said. 'Anyway, I wasn't particularly worried because it could

61

have been me or a hundred others, I live thirty miles from where it all happened and I'm damn sure I didn't leave any fingerprints.

'Then, this morning at work, I got a call from a bloke I used to know among the saboteurs, back where I came from. He and his girl are almost the only ones in that rabble who know me. They were out doing a bit of disruption yesterday and there was some organised retaliation. Nothing violent, unfortunately, or they could have made some capital out of it. But one or two of our friends will land in court. The Hunt seem to have brought in a lot of help, and somebody who recognised one of them thinks they were soldiers from the barracks. Anyway, they attached themselves to the saboteurs and at a given moment they each produced those Photo-fit pictures and made some insinuating remark. My friend says that his girl let Mary's name slip before he could stop her.'

'That could be serious,' Mrs Colcarth said. 'If they get onto you through her . . .'

'Don't worry, I wouldn't drop any of you in the shit,' Mike said. 'I don't mind standing up and being counted on my own. But it won't happen. I asked for the day off, dashed round and found Mary just coming out of her dad's house. The rest of the family were at work but she's out of a job, which made it easier. Nobody'd been near her yet.

'I told her what had happened and reminded her that she was as deeply implicated as anybody.

'The upshot was that she left a note for her family to say that she was off job-hunting in London, and I moved her into my place. She thinks I'm going to marry her. I might even do it, if I get a rush of blood to the vital organs.

'She's getting her hair cut and tinted just now, and buying some girlish clothes instead of those punkish unisex outfits. With a change of make-up, and so far from her home, I don't see anybody recognising her.'

Mrs Colcarth was twisting her head to look at him disapprovingly. But, after all, it was his ruthlessness which had made him most useful to the group. 'I suppose it's all right,' she said. 'You may have to keep her out of circulation for some time, but I don't suppose you'll mind that. Have you seen the newspaper?'

Mike glanced down and nodded. 'That's the place I was telling you about,' he said. 'It's almost on your doorstep, Mrs C. What have you been up to?'

Eric Foulkes sniggered and tried to turn it into one of his frequent sniffs.

'I?' Mrs Colcarth said in awful tones. 'I distinctly said that I wanted the place left alone. If the police come around asking questions, it may come out that I told the proprietor that he ought to be skinned alive to atone for his sins. That might start them looking into the times of my comings and goings, and who I go to meet. Do you know anything about this?'

'God, no. It's the only fur farm for fifty miles. Somebody was bound to take it on sooner or later. I hope they get away with it. If that man took a heart attack because of the excitement, the law may go harder on them. Well, at least he can't tell anybody about your tiff with him.'

'Do you have any idea who the Justice for Animals League are?' Mrs Colcarth asked.

'No idea. If they were affiliated to the ALF, we'd have been told before they took action on our ground. Probably an offshoot of the Animal Rights Militia. Good luck to them, I say. Mink have as much right to life and freedom as anyone else, and if a fur-farmer happened to get in the way it serves him right for being in such a foul trade.'

'All right,' Mrs Colcarth said irritably. 'Don't preach

to the converted. Listen while we tell you what we've been deciding.'

Mike shrugged. He caught Eric's eye in the driving mirror and they exchanged a wink. He listened carefully. 'I'm game,' he said at the end.

'Do we bring the fringe members in – students and oddballs?' Eric asked.

Lucy nudged her husband. 'I suggest not,' Hugh said. 'Not unless the plan can't work without extra bodies. This is a bit too heavy. Students tend to carry on as if we were perpetrating a huge practical joke, and this year's batch seem to be overgrown schoolboys. We should handle this ourselves if we can.'

'For once, I'm inclined to agree with our friend in the rear,' Mike said. 'The least idiotic of the bunch is that goon with the protruding ears, Terry Janson, and he doesn't have the sense to obey a court order. He got himself caught disrupting the Hunt while under an injunction to cease and desist. He's not going to be nice to know for a while. I told him not to come near any of us until further notice.'

'There you are,' Hugh said.

'I'd have liked to think we could manage for ourselves, with some help from my little friend,' Mike went on. 'But we can't. If we're going to get full mileage from this little caper, we need a competent photographer with us. And while Terry may have a single figure IQ, he's damn good with a camera. His company can't contaminate us in the dark, and between us we should be able to control his wilder urges.'

'If he gets caught again,' Lucy said, 'they'll really clobber him.'

'Oh what a shame!' said Mike. 'Dearie, dearie me!'

As always, the telephone made a startling intrusion into the quiet of the day. Angela Broderick jerked nervously

and then reminded herself that it was easier to answer
the phone than the door-bell. She got up, hurrying out
of habit in case the caller rang off, followed the back of
the settee as far as the side-table, and felt for the
instrument. It eluded her for a few seconds – sometimes
she thought that the damned thing could walk – and
then materialised under her hand.

As she repeated her number, the rapid bleeps of a
pay-phone over-rode her. Then the caller's voice came
on, a girl's voice or a woman's, clear and well-spoken
despite a trace of the local accent.

'Mrs Broderick?'

'Speaking,' Angela said.

'Are you the Mrs Broderick who ... ?' The voice
shied away from the specific.

It was not the first such call. 'Who wants to know?'
she asked tiredly.

'I just wanted to tell you how sorry I was,' the voice
said. 'We all are. Nothing like that was meant to
happen. It was supposed to be a gesture, nothing more
than that.'

Angela drew in a deep breath as she realised who was
on the line. 'And you'd feel better about it if I said that I
forgave you?' she suggested bitterly.

'I suppose I would.' The voice sounded thoughtful.
'But that isn't why I rang.'

'Why, then?'

'To say we were sorry. It can't help much, but it
might help a bit. And to ask if there was anything I
could do ... to help, or to make amends. I do mean it,'
the voice added.

'You mean like coming into hospital with me and
having our corneas exchanged?'

There was a silence on the line. Angela waited, the
receiver quivering against her ear. She expected her
caller to hang up and relieve her of the stress to which

65

the discussion was subjecting her. But the voice spoke again and she was amazed to realise that her bitter sarcasm was being taken seriously.

'I don't think they'd do it,' said the voice. 'Not between living people. Would they?'

'No, of course not,' Angela said impatiently. She could hear her own voice becoming shrill. The existence of an individual to focus her anger, even one as remote as an anonymous voice on the phone, brought her buried resentment to the surface. 'And you wouldn't do it, so don't try to pretend that you would. Why don't you come and give me a hand with some housework? It doesn't matter how good you are at it, just as long as you can see what you're doing.'

'Please try not to be so angry. I'll come and help, if you'll promise, on your word of honour, that you won't call the police or anything like that.'

'I could promise,' Angela said. 'And I could keep the promise if only I could see to do to you what you've done to me. You bitch!' she added.

There was another pause before the voice spoke again. 'I meant to make things better,' it said gently, 'but I've made them worse. I'm sorry. I'll stop bothering you now, but first I'll tell you this. I won't stop fighting for the sake of the animals, because what's right is still right. But I'll do my best to see that nobody ever gets hurt again.'

'Like the man at the fur farm?'

'That wasn't us,' the voice said quickly. 'Anyway, I hope things are better for you soon. I won't bother you again. Goodbye.'

The receiver suddenly uttered the dialling tone. The caller was gone. Angela would have liked to call back some of her words, even to try to establish a rapport with whoever-it-was, but it was too late. She felt the tears coming. She groped her way back to her chair and gave herself up to them.

At the other end of the town, Mary Jennings left the call-box and walked towards her new home. Like Angela, she felt the need for tears, but she blinked them away. Her chin was up. At least she felt a little better for having tried.

NINE

Major Craythorne's military experience had attuned him to modern methods of communication. He seemed to live much of his professional life on various forms of telephone or radio. But in private he disliked the telephone. Messages passed over it with less than military precision became garbled, and nobody ever called one back.

So, failing at first try to reach Inspector Cheyne on the phone, he seized on the next excuse to drive into the city and seek out the inspector in person.

Brief discussion with the desk sergeant, coupled with a flat refusal to see anyone else, soon established that the inspector was out of his office. He was at the mortuary of the City Hospital but not, Jonathan gathered, among the cadavers because the sergeant was obliging enough to ascertain by radio that the inspector would be pleased to meet the major at the door of the Pathology Department in fifteen minutes' time.

The inspector was already waiting outside the building when Jonathan drove up and he walked to meet the car. He was looking pale and drawing on a cigarette for comfort. 'We'll have one of our strolls,' he suggested.

'Do you suppose anyone would object to the dog?'

'Probably. But I don't suppose they'd do anything about it. And, if they do, you seem to have the technique for dealing with them.'

'That's all right, then.' Jonathan allowed Shona out of the car and they set off around the paths between carpets of grass too severe to be called lawns. 'Good of you to see me.'

'Relieved to see you,' the inspector said. 'Attending autopsies is part of the job but I don't think any of us

68

ever get used to it. Pathologists are always so cheerful and matter-of-fact about their grisly business that it turns me up. And they never seem to notice the smell. I was glad of an excuse to get out for a bit. And what's your news?'

When Jonathan explained, the inspector looked both shocked and amused. 'You had no business meddling in police work,' he said without severity, and mollified his words further by adding, 'Very well done! Mary Jennings, eh? We'll see what that young lady can tell us.'

'My chap pointed out the house to me,' Jonathan said. 'Fourteen, Wellbrook Terrace. And the best of luck to you! She may possibly be in a talkative mood. My sister had a phone-call which probably came from her. Unfortunately, Angela got upset about it and lost her temper. Otherwise she might have been able to coax some more information out of her.'

Jonathan repeated the gist of the call, as nearly as his sister had managed to remember it, while the inspector rested his notebook on the side of a parked ambulance and wrote steadily. Cheyne's only comment was a grunt.

'What progress have you made?' Jonathan asked. 'Or can't you tell me?'

'If I'd made any progress up to two minutes ago, I probably couldn't have told you. We've had no luck with the shop-assistant, by the way – Croll seems to have him brain-washed. Getting a name may be the breakthrough we needed. Until now, it's been like running in treacle. It's like this. There's what you might call a three-tier structure,' the inspector went on. He was not usually a communicative man, but the alternative to talking was a return to the hated post-mortem room. 'Under one or two umbrella organisations like the Animal Protection Alliance, you have some perfectly sincere and quite legal campaigning bodies like the

RSPCA, Animal Aid, Greenpeace and Friends of the Earth. You may or may not consider them to be cranks, but they have something to say and a perfect right to say it.

'And then you have illegal activists like the Animal Liberation Front, Animal Rights Militia and three regional Animal Liberation Leagues. Those are the dangerous ones. They'll kill somebody, one of these days, if they haven't already done so.

'It's impossible to prove that the second and third tiers know each other or have any common membership, and if the legitimate bodies know any names among the illegal ones they've never been known to divulge them. Similarly, as you worked out for yourself, there must be links with the Hunt Saboteurs and the Hunt Retribution Squad. The problem is that most of the activists are youngsters, students mostly, and there's a constant turnover of membership as they grow out of it all. There must be a hard core of adults giving continuity, though, but they keep their heads very low. Those are the ones we want.'

They walked through the thin sunshine in silence for a few minutes, under the envying eyes of patients in the ward blocks. Their path brought them back to the carpark.

'I'd better be getting back to my duties,' Jonathan said.

'And I to my autopsy,' the inspector said distastefully. 'With a little luck, the more revolting stages will be over by now.'

'Interesting case?'

'Not very. But it might throw some light on the case of your sister. It's the man who died during the raid at the fur farm. Your sister's caller may have denied responsibility but I'd bet on a connection.'

'Geographically speaking, I thought that that was outside your area.'

'It was. But, because of the possible link with this case, I was invited to sit in.' The inspector paused and then decided to spin out his respite from the autopsy. 'It looks like an ordinary heart attack brought on by over-exertion.'

'You sound as if you had your doubts,' Jonathan suggested.

'I had, but I suppose they're either groundless or impossible to prove. The man had had his heart listened to within the last few weeks and was passed as fit. He was known to have both guts and a temper – just the type to "have a go". And the yard was muddy. The footprints were clear to be seen and they mill around in a manner strongly suggesting a fight. Well, that could have brought on a heart attack, I suppose. But it surprises me that the pathologist's found no signs of violence so far. From the footprints, I could have sworn that at least one blow had been struck.'

Jonathan might lack knowledge about criminal investigation, but he was a much travelled man and he moved in circles wherein various aspects of violence were common coin. 'Have you ever heard of a blow called the "Singapore"?' he asked.

The inspector looked at him in surprise.

'The original Chinese name translates as "Rock Crusher",' Jonathan said, 'although no great strength's needed. It was adopted from the Chinese by the Singapore police, for use when set on, because it's a very effective attack-stopper but leaves no obvious signs of violence. It's a blow delivered with a folding hand, up under the ribs. It sends a double pulse of great pressure through the blood vessels. The valves of the heart rupture and the victim dies too quickly for bruising to develop.'

'I had heard of such a thing,' the inspector said, 'but I put it in the same bracket as the novelist's little-known Oriental poison. You're not pulling my leg?'

Jonathan gave the inspector a playful dig in the ribs. 'I'll demonstrate if you like.'

The other shied away. 'If there really is such a thing, you can keep well away from me. Demonstrate on my sergeant.'

'Believe me, it's real,' Jonathan said. He was not going to tell the inspector so, but while undercover in Belfast he had saved his own life with the blow. 'I don't know much about forensic medicine, but you might suggest that they look for signs of tissue damage just under the fork of the ribs.'

The inspector sat on the wing of Jonathan's car and scowled at an inoffensive sparrow. 'I'll do that. But I have difficulty associating such sophisticated violence with our animal-lovers. What sort of person would know about such a thing?'

'Almost anybody who'd had a friend in one of the rougher branches of the armed forces. And don't forget, Inspector, your charming animal-lovers blinded my sister.'

TEN

The business to which Mike Underhill grudgingly spared his time, in exchange for remuneration which he considered to be less than his due, customarily dealt with the Microchipshop and had urgent need of a fresh box of computer-paper. Mike went in his grumbling old Escort to fetch it.

Quite by chance, Councillor Croll was coming out of the shop as Mike parked his car at the door. Croll walked quickly to the car. Mike wound down his window.

'Your neck's on the block,' Croll said. 'Don't hang around here. Meet me in the small bar at the Dog and Grapes.'

Mike had more sense than to argue, and he was quick-witted. 'I want a box of computer-paper,' he said. 'The usual.'

'It would be something heavy! All right, I'll bring it.'

They met five minutes later in the small back room of the pub. They had the place to themselves. 'You owe me a drink as well as the cash for the paper,' Croll said. 'I'll take a whisky.'

Mike ordered two whiskies. 'If this is just a gimmick to get a drink off me—'

'It isn't.'

'Then what's the panic?'

Croll waited until the fat barmaid had delivered the drinks and left. 'There was a policeman in the shop the other day with a Photo-fit picture which couldn't have been anybody but you. He seemed sure that you'd been a customer. Know what it's about?'

Mike paused before answering. But he was already vulnerable. It could hardly matter if Croll knew a little

73

more. 'The ALF,' he said. 'That bitch who went and blinded herself. She wasn't meant to. She used the stuff before the warnings took effect.'

'I thought that might be it. Young Pea-brain could probably have put them onto your employers when he got around to remembering the invoices. He was beginning to spread himself to one of the local law, but I choked him off.'

Mike swallowed. Quixotic but illegal activities from the safe anonymity of a secret group had been a kick, but the danger of revelation made his stomach churn. He pacified it with whisky. 'How did they trace me to your shop?' he asked.

'God knows. But I can tell you something. There was another man hanging around the shop. Young, tall, well-dressed, very tidy. Walked with a spring in his step. Strong smell of peppermints. An arrogant and toffee-nosed bastard. He listened to every word and then walked out without buying anything.' Croll reddened at the memory. 'I was curious. I went to the door. I heard the copper speak to him. He called him "Major".'

'There's a hell of a lot of majors around.'

'This was no retired old buffer hanging onto a wartime rank,' Croll said. 'This one's serving. And how many majors would there be at the barracks? Not that it'd help you to know him. He didn't look the kind you could buy off or get round with a sob-story.'

'Maybe, or maybe not,' Mike said thoughtfully. 'According to the papers, the woman's brother who made the purchase was a major. Name of Craythorne. I think I passed him in the shop door, which shows how close it was. He certainly smelled of peppermints. But he looked a proper Wally.'

It was Croll's turn to sound thoughtful. 'A man in the club was talking about a Major Craythorne just last night,' he said. 'If it's the same man, don't underestimate him. He wanders around seemingly in a daze, looking as if he'd be lost if he wandered ten yards from his mother, but behind that front he's a tough. He's been everywhere. He's on the IRA's wanted list. In the Falklands, I'm told that he jumped on an Argie sniper who'd shot two of his men after waving a white flag, and he filleted him like a kipper. Walk gently around that character would be my advice.'

'What's it to you, anyway? Why are you telling me this?'

'I'm sympathetic to Animal Rights.'

'You're sympathetic to Councillor Croll and his political ambitions. I heard you'd got your sights set on Parliament. You think there's votes in it?' Mike asked cynically.

Croll took the question in all seriousness. 'Not in vivisection directly,' he said. 'There are no votes in reminding the public about something it's made up its mind it'd rather not know about. But that, my young friend, is why a lot of votes could go up the spout if I had to give evidence against you.'

'You could be a useful friend to us,' Mike said. 'Do some good for once. We need another voice in the Commons.'

'Well, count on my vote but not my voice. Espousing lost causes is political suicide. I could do with the animal-lovers' vote, though. I thought of taking up opposition to hunting and shooting.'

'And fishing?'

'No,' Croll said frankly. 'There's too many of the buggers fish. Are you a member of the Hunt Saboteurs?'

'I used to be.'

'Have another drink – my turn this time – and you can fill me in on the arguments.'

★ ★ ★

Mike returned to work, but his mind was not on his job. Pursuit had become real and frightening.

He had affected to despise the rat-race and to make humorous apologies for his entry into it, but now he could admit to himself that he valued his place in the hierarchy and the modest purchasing-power which it brought him. In the abstract, the vision of standing up for a count of one had seemed exhilarating; but the prospect of disgrace, prosecution and a return to the unemployment line brought him to the point of physical nausea.

What Councillor Croll had told him about Craythorne had rocked his world. No longer was he opposed by a faceless and impotent society. The enemy now was a soldier, highly trained, observant, evidently ruthless and out to avenge a blinded sister.

He forced himself to stay calm and to evaluate the danger. If the worst came to the worst, what was the evidence against him? The busy chemist and his harassed assistant were no danger – he had forced himself to visit the shop again and they had served him, with no sign of recognition. And the Photo-fit face would not be good evidence without the testimony of the man who had created it. Without the major, in fact, he was free and clear.

From what Croll had said, the IRA would be delighted to know where their infiltrator had disappeared to and to take retributive action. But they might move too slowly. In any case, he had no idea how to contact any of their members.

He slumped over his console. His colleagues glanced at him with sympathy and a little envy. Clearly he was suffering from the after-effects of one of the orgies at which he sometimes hinted.

Should he keep his head down and hope for the best? No, that would be passive acceptance which was foreign to him. Indeed, it was the passive acceptance of fate by the animal world which had spurred him to action on its behalf. Worse, his nerves would never stand the suspense. He must take action, if only in flight.

But no. Flight would mean the abandonment of everything he had achieved or hoped to achieve. It might also be evidence of guilt. Stick it out, he told himself. Think your way through it.

Perhaps . . . He pushed the thought away but it kept creeping back. Perhaps the Justice for Animals League should make one more strike.

At the Wildfowl Park, Mrs Colcarth found the office-and-shop deserted, which surprised her. Even in winter, there was usually somebody, the warden or one of his helpers, ready to admit visitors, give them information or sell them books or souvenirs. She waited impatiently for a few minutes, pursing her lips and frowning. This was no way to treat a valued patroness.

At last she decided that the mountain would, for once, have to go in search of Mohammed. She entered through the gate in the high perimeter fence and then, picking her way carefully in unsuitable shoes, followed the sawdust paths between the low fences of the wildfowl enclosures.

The widespread areas of the pens seemed remarkably empty. Even the small ponds held only a handful of ducks. With difficulty, she spotted a few geese, huddled nervously under bushes in the naturalistic habitat which had consumed so much devoted labour in its creation out of a tract of barren land.

She found the warden busy with two helpers around a large hole. She thought vaguely that he must be making another pond. He looked up as she approached and straightened his back. She thought that he looked haggard. But that was no excuse for telephoning a message which invited her to call and then not being around to meet her.

'What is it this time?' she asked.

Morrow looked at her curiously. She was essentially a selfish and inward-looking woman, blind to anything which did not affect her own comfort or offend her prejudices, but sometimes her self-centredness passed the bounds of reason. 'Look for yourself,' he suggested.

For the first time, Mrs Colcarth realised that the bottom of the pit was heaped with dead ducks and geese, and that one of the helpers was bringing a fresh supply of corpses. There was blood on the plumage but whatever had killed them did not seem to have fed.

'Whatever happened?' she asked, and she added quickly, 'It can't have been Sam. He was in all night.'

'Mink,' Morrow said savagely. 'They came down one of the watercourses. I thought that we had the culverts adequately netted, but those little devils can get in anywhere. I'm afraid we're almost back to Square One, where we were four years ago.'

'How awful for you,' she said.

He shrugged. 'It's worse for these poor things,' he said. 'It'll have been some of the mink let loose by those maniacs from the Justice for Animals League. Just another name for the Animal Liberation Front, I suppose. Maniacs,' he repeated.

Mrs Colcarth thought that it might be dangerous to let her indignation show. 'Surely that's a harsh judgement,' she said carefully. 'They seem to be perfectly sincere people, trying to make a point which can't be made any other way. They could hardly have known that something like this would happen.'

The warden's distress was too deep for any more pandering to this silly woman. It was time that she faced some facts. 'I said maniacs and I meant it,' he retorted.

'Putting poisoned things on shop shelves, and letting loose these vicious little killers. It's the height of irresponsibility. Both times, they must have known the harm they could do.'

She had been on the point of offering him a cheque to help with restocking the Wildfowl Park, but she put it out of her mind. 'It may be tragic,' she said, 'but I don't think that you have any right to condemn these people out of hand. If they're against cruelty, they deserve our support.'

The warden recovered some of his temper. 'Nobody's in favour of cruelty,' he said patiently. 'But I don't equate being against cruelty with attacking medical experiments and letting killers loose on our wildlife. We have legal and democratic processes for righting wrongs. If Parliament won't legislate, then it means that the bulk of the electorate don't wish it.'

'Parliament doesn't legislate because people don't know or don't think.' Mrs Colcarth's voice, at full volume, came back in an echo from one of the hills. 'At least these people are helping to draw the public's attention to the terrible wrongs which are being done,' she boomed. She worked a little raw emotion into her voice. It always went down well with those who were sympathetically inclined, and surely Mr Morrow of all people had to be among the angels. 'Do you realise that those mink were being kept in small cages, just to be killed and skinned? Do you realise the tortures that some animals are made to suffer in the name of so-called science, to bring more and more drugs into the world that people would be better off without and so make money for the drug companies?' She paused for a deep breath. 'And do you realise that there are still sadists in the world who actually kill things for fun?'

This was too much. Morrow enjoyed a day out with a dog and a gun himself. But still he held his temper in check. 'You love our countryside, don't you?' he asked.

Mrs Colcarth looked around. Even in its winter browns, half-naked through the bare trees, the undulating landscape was familiar and dear. She heaved a deep sigh, imposing a strain on her corsetry which that masterpiece barely withstood. 'I adore it,' she said simply and believed what she said.

'And you believe that, if all hunting and shooting were stopped, you'd have a countryside full of birds and animals, all living happily together?'

She began to realise that something was wrong. 'Why not? Think how tame your birds usually are.'

'This is an unnatural, protected environment. But our open countryside,' said Morrow, 'is the result of a thousand years of man's involvement with hunting for his meat. The whole pattern of farming and forestry is strongly influenced by that one fact. If there were no sport, prairie farming would take over here as it has elsewhere.'

'But—'

'No, let me finish. You've had your say, let me have mine. I'm an ecologist, Mrs Colcarth, and I know what I'm talking about. Our wildlife owes its state to the fact that man is a hunter. Shooting interests put far more into the conservation of wildlife than all other interests put together. They improve and retain the habitat, Mrs Colcarth, and they feed the wildlife, and above all they control predators. In short, they do the major part of maintaining what you naïvely think of as a balance of nature. Do away with shooting, Mrs Colcarth, and you'll do away with songbirds in much of our countryside at the same time.'

'You've no right to say such things,' she said loudly, hoping to drown his voice. Morrow's two assistants were listening avidly but she did not care.

'Why not?' Morrow asked. 'If I accept that you've a

right to your opinions, can't you accept that I've a right to mine?'

'No. Because they're wrong and immoral. They deny all that's good in man, and in animals too. You shouldn't be allowed.'

'Can't you accept that wildlife is . . . just that? Wild. It's a constant scene of predation, and man is the least of the predators. Life in the wild is a battle against starvation and predation. Those are wildlife's enemies. Not man. But I'm not getting through to you, am I?'

'No you are not. And if you brought me all this way just to read me a lecture and to show me a lot of beastly bodies, then I'm going.'

'Come this way,' Morrow said sadly. He was sorry to see the end of what had been a difficult relationship but one which had been of great benefit to his beloved wildfowl collection. But then he managed to find a little comfort. If it had to end, at least it could end on a note which would afford him great pleasure. It shouldn't, but it would.

He led the way over to a place near the perimeter fence, where five cage-traps were ranged side by side. Each held the body of a bird – woodpigeon in this case, because he had been lucky with the gun – together with the corpse of at least one mink, furred and beautiful even in death but with needle-sharp fangs bared in the last, defiant snarl. In the end trap was also a large bundle of black fur.

'I'm afraid that a cat got into one of the traps first,' Morrow said. 'Three of the mink followed it in and made a meal of it. But if Sam was at home all night, it can't be him, can it?'

Mrs Colcarth turned and walked away without a word. Cats could be replaced.

Morrow began to take the bodies out of the traps. He kept the mink for skinning – the pelts would go some

81

way towards replacing the losses. But he threw the cat into the pit alongside his dead birds. He was glad to lose sight of it as the hole was filled. The cat, although an old enemy, had been on his conscience. It had been alone and alive in the trap when he had first found it. The temptation to transfer mink from other cage-traps had been too much for him.

Mrs Colcarth returned home fuming. Like many another person of an inflexible turn of mind, argument only strengthened her opinions and renewed her determination. She wanted to lash out; and, if a blow were to be struck, Gillespie and Baker would make a worthwhile target.

ELEVEN

If Jonathan Craythorne noticed the Ford Escort which, for the second day running, hung on his tail three cars behind, it was only with the same subconscious fragment of his mind which saw without seeing the buildings and streets and river and sky. His attention was elsewhere. He sucked one of his eternal peppermints – the hankering for a smoke was always strongest when he was driving – and dropped his hand to Shona's head. The setter responded with a quick thump of her tail. She was only allowed to travel on the floor in front of the passenger's seat when her master felt the need of her company.

Jonathan eased the big car through the streets to the carpark which he usually favoured. As usual, it was barely half-full. He left the driver's window slightly down for Shona's sake – a considerate habit which he would gruffly explain away on the grounds that he disliked coming back to 'a carful of doggyfart'.

One small errand on behalf of his colonel was completed within a few minutes. He found himself near the police station. On an impulse, he went in and asked for Inspector Cheyne.

The inspector met him in one of the interview rooms. 'You seem to be my only source of information,' he said. 'Every other soul with a concern in the case has gone either dumb or abusive. Have you brought me any more goodies?'

'You're too greedy,' Jonathan said. 'I called in to find out what use you'd made of my other titbits.'

'Not a lot. The girl, Mary Jennings, seems to have done a bunk, so that line's at an impasse until we can trace her. Always assuming that we're onto the right

Mary Jennings, of course. But she'd been referring to her boyfriend as Mike, so we can be hopeful.'

'And did your pathologist follow up my other suggestion?'

'He followed it up.'

'And?'

'And all I can say at the present is to thank you for your public-spirited co-operation.' The inspector's meaning was unmistakable.

'That's all?'

'That's the lot.'

'And you're quite sure that whoever was first on the scene didn't try to restart his heart by thumping his chest?'

'That was the first question the pathologist asked. They say not.'

'How very interesting,' Jonathan said. He left the station, walking slowly and thoughtfully.

In the Escort, Mary Jennings was a puzzled and questioning passenger until Mike Underhill cursed her into silence. Then she could only sit, telling herself over and over again that she loved him despite, or perhaps because of, his domination. Even so, when he was like this, riding the crest of his fury, she was afraid, as much for him as for herself. Nothing and nobody, not even reason, would stand unscathed between him and his goal, whatever his goal might be. He had refused to tell her his plan. She could only guess; and none of her guesses gave her any comfort.

The big Volvo was easily followed. Mike parked four slots away from it and gave a grunt of satisfaction. The major was a creature of habit. As on the previous day, he had left his peppermints on the dash and the driver's window slightly open. This was going to be easy.

'Why are we just sitting here?' Mary dared to ask.

He nearly cursed her again, but he needed her help. She would be no use in the state of sullen resentment to which he had found he could easily reduce her. Sometimes it suited his purpose, but not now. 'I think that couple with the Vauxhall are going to move out,' he said.

'But why—?'

'You'll see.'

The couple with the Vauxhall were damnably slow in putting their Christmas shopping away. They fitted it into the boot like a Chinese puzzle, adjusting the load to be sure that the heavier parcels were at the bottom and the more fragile above. They were satisfied at last. They got inside and adjusted seats and mirrors before driving off, quite unaware of the blast of hatred projected towards them from three cars away.

Mike jerked the Escort forward with a yelp of protesting tyres, swung round and backed into a position beside the Volvo's offside. He looked around. The few morning shoppers were paying no attention to them.

'I can't get out,' Mary said plaintively. 'My door doesn't have room to open.'

'You don't have to get out. Wind your window down.'

'But why? Mike, what are we—?'

'Just do as I say,' Mike told her in a cold, flat voice. 'Reach across and grab that bag of sweets. Your hands are smaller than mine.'

Mary tried. 'My arm won't go far enough through,' she said.

Mike had tried to think of every contingency. He produced a pair of kitchen tongs. 'Use these.'

Using the tongs, Mary secured the paper bag and passed it to Mike. He dropped it into one of the door-pockets and from the same place produced an almost identical bag of peppermints. He shook a few sweets out into his hand so that the fullness of the bags would match. 'Put this where the other ones were,' he said urgently.

'But Mike—'

'Just do it!'

'But why . . . ? Mike, what were you doing to them the other night?'

His patience and his temper went altogether. He put his hand behind him and it came out with a horn-handled sheath-knife. The silver blade looked sharp enough for skinning an elephant and the point was too fine to see. He held it in front of her face, so close that she thought he was going to slice her flesh.

'Do what I tell you, at once, no questions,' he said. 'Or else.' His face was a stranger's, blotched red and white and with feverish eyes. She would never have believed that so much menace could be compressed into so small a space.

Panic-stricken, she tried to follow his instructions; but, in her fear, she fumbled. The tongs sprang apart. 'It's fallen down inside,' she whispered.

He punched his own knee. 'You stupid little cow! It'll have to do. Give me the tongs.'

'They fell down too.'

'Jesus sodding Christ! They have my prints all over them.' Hardly taking time to think, Mike started the engine and shot the car across the gangway into a slot opposite. 'Come with me.'

She followed him back on shaking legs.

'Force your arm in and open the door.'

She tried. 'I can't,' she said. 'It's too narrow.'

'You must. Nothing was ever more important. Take your coat off.'

She removed her thin coat and dropped it on the

tarmac. 'It's still too narrow.'

'Push like hell.'

She tried again until she thought that her skin would rip. 'It won't go. And, Mike, somebody'll see us.'

'Nobody's looking.'

With the strength of desperation she forced her forearm into the gap. 'I still can't reach,' she wailed. 'Anyway, I don't know how it opens.'

He looked round for a tool, anything with which he could force or smash a window, and then froze. 'Oh God! Here he is, coming back. Make yourself scarce.'

Mike walked quickly away along the row of cars, leaving her with her forearm jammed between the glass and the frame. Without seeming to hurry, he had faded into the background within a few seconds. He paused at a refuse-bin to dispose of the handful of surplus peppermints. Then he was gone.

She extricated her arm with a frantic heave. She had no wish to rejoin Mike in his present mood. She was about to scurry across the carpark, at right-angles to Jonathan's approach, when a last glimpse of the car's interior froze her mind and her body.

Shona, during her master's frequent absences on duty, was quite accustomed to living in his car and to the presence of strangers around it. She had lain still, inconspicuous against the russet carpet and as uninterested in their activities as she would have been in the comings and goings of the soldiers at the barracks. She knew better than to touch the sweets while they were up on the dash; but, by long-standing custom, those which were dropped on the carpet were hers to take. She sat up and began to feast on her favourite delicacy.

Mary looked with desperation after Mike but he had vanished. Anyway, he would not have helped. She stooped to the gap above the glass. 'Leave it!' she said. 'Sit. Stop!' And when Shona paid no attention, 'No!'

That last word is part of any dog's small vocabulary. Shona hesitated. But she was accustomed to obeying the voices of men. Mary's voice she associated with those of the nieces, who could be disobeyed with impunity. She snapped up a peppermint, swallowed it whole and went after another.

'Sit,' Mary screeched. Shona threw her an impatient glance. She was already sitting.

Mary was wringing her hands when Jonathan Craythorne arrived behind her. 'What's going on?' he demanded.

'Oh, please,' Mary said. 'Do something. Your dog's eating sweets and I think they may have been poisoned.' Her duty done, as she saw it, she snatched up her coat and prepared to hurry off.

Despite his concern for Shona, Jonathan was not going to let Mary fade away. He grabbed her wrist and pulled her round the car while with his other hand he fumbled for the key. Mary found herself bundled into the passenger seat and Shona was lifted by the scruff of the neck and draped across her knees.

'Hang onto her,' the major said. 'Don't let her take any more. You know your way around here? Direct me to the nearest vet. Quickly, girl.' He was already in the driver's seat, scooping up the sweet-bag and stowing it away in the glove-compartment.

Now that somebody was in charge, Mary could begin to pull herself together. 'Left in the street,' she said, 'and left again at the lights.' She fished for a handkerchief, blew her nose and dabbed at her face.

Jonathan swung out, stealing time to look at his passengers. Shona looked puzzled but bright-eyed. Mary's face found an echo somewhere in Jonathan's subconscious.

'You're sure they were poisoned?' he asked.

'Not positive. I think so.'

'Why do you think it?'

'I can't see any other reason why . . . somebody . . . was doing what he was doing. Please, don't ask me any more.'

They were stopped at the lights. He would have slipped round to the left, but there was a car halted in front of them. He looked again at Mary, trying to fit her face into those which had been outside the chemist's shop. The girl outside the pharmacy, he was sure, had been wearing leather and gaudy ear-rings and her hair had been longer, but the high cheekbones, short nose and full lips were the same.

'You're Mary Jennings, aren't you?' he said.

It was a guess, but he knew that it was a good one while she was still denying it. The puzzle began to fall into place. Shona's head had gone down and she was panting. Please, dear God, he thought, don't let it work so quickly! The lights changed, the car in front moved off and he hauled the Volvo, wallowing, round the corner.

'Which way now?'

'Along to the church and then right.'

'What was the poison? The vet will want to know.'

'I don't know. But I saw a packet of Rodentine, it might be that. What . . . what are you going to do?'

Jonathan turned right at the church. 'I'm going to leave her,' he said, 'for the best attention the vet can give her, and take you to the police station to make a statement.'

'Please, no,' she said. The tears came again. 'I've done all I can for you.'

'You must see that I can't leave that boyfriend of yours running around trying to kill people,' he said in exasperation. 'Where now?'

'Right along almost to the end,' she said. 'I've seen a vet's plate. It may not have been the nearest one, but it's

89

the only one I know. You don't understand,' she added bitterly, stumbling over the words in her anxiety. 'It's not just Mike. The others will be depending on my help at the factory tonight. I can't let everybody down. I've got to be there. I've just got to. It's too important. We must make people see that all this torturing of helpless animals has got to be stopped.'

He concentrated on sliding the car through a narrowing gap. Shona jerked suddenly and vomited over Mary's lap and onto the floor. The smell filled the car.

He could see the vet's sign. There was no room to park. He swung left into a narrow lane and stopped.

'Come in with me.'

She shrank down in her seat. 'Please, no! I don't think I could bear it.'

'If I waste time on you,' he said, 'my dog will die and then I'll never forgive you. I'll follow you wherever you go. At least promise me you'll wait in the car until I come out.'

'I promise,' she said. 'Honestly.' He looked into her face and thought that she meant it.

He ran round the car and gathered the now writhing dog into his arms. As he hurried through the surgery door, an Escort slowed to a halt behind the Volvo.

TWELVE

When Jonathan came out of the surgery, there was no sign of the girl. He was only mildly surprised. It had been a toss-up whether fear and her promise would outweigh her duty to her group. He stood, leaning on the car's roof, and breathed the fresh air for a few moments while he gathered his thoughts.

Shona, heavily sedated, had been asleep when he left. The vet had at first wanted to put her out of her misery, but at Jonathan's insistence had instead washed out her stomach, injected antidotes and had ended by promising, without any great air of hope, that everything possible would be done.

He opened the car door. From force of habit, he was about to look for a peppermint when the smell of dog's vomit reminded him. He recovered the sweet-bag, closed the door and set off on foot.

While he walked, he cleared his mind of its anxiety and tried to think out his line of action. Inspector Cheyne was not a hide-bound copper.... But no. Given an attempted murder, he would have to treat it as business for the police exclusively.

The nearest hotel was the Great Southern. The bar, with its broad windows giving a panoramic view of the river, was open but quiet. He had a brandy to wash away the aftertaste and he bought cigarettes. It would be a long time before he could fancy a peppermint again.

He took his change into one of the well-fitted phone-boxes and lit a cigarette, drawing luxuriously on the longed-for smoke. It made his head swim at first.

His first call was to Gillespie and Baker. The General Manager, he was told, was abroad. He asked who was in charge.

'Dr Whelks,' said the girl's voice.

'The Director of Research? Just the man,' Jonathan said. 'Can you put me on to him?'

Dr Whelks's voice came on a few moments later. 'Good morning, Major.'

'It is,' Jonathan said, 'and I don't want to spoil it for you, but I believe that our friends have it in mind to visit your factory tonight.'

'You have grounds for this belief?'

'Some. Does anybody else have an animal research facility around here?'

'Only the University and one consulting lab,' Whelks said.

'My informant let slip that her friends would need her "at the factory". That would be you?'

'I can't think of another. You've told the police?'

'Not yet,' Jonathan said. 'I'll have to report some other matters. But it occurred to me that a police guard might not be the best answer. It might do no more than postpone the visit.'

Whelks was slow to answer. Jonathan could sense the scientific brain sifting like a computer through the options. 'I can hardly call out the army,' Whelks said.

'Of course not. But I had been thinking of taking some of the men on a night training exercise. . . .'

Again the pause. 'I like it,' Whelks said suddenly. 'I think we can do business. Provided that we do it my way.'

'That's understood,' Jonathan said. 'I won't tell the police about the few words she let slip, then.'

They spoke for a few more minutes.

He lit another cigarette. After his long abstinence, the smoke was almost as bracing as the brandy. His second call was to the barracks, to his old friend and sparring-partner Sergeant-Major Heather.

'Heather?'

92

'Major, Sir?' The sergeant-major would never have bestowed the double salutation on any other officer.

'I have a bit of trouble on my hands,' the major said, 'and I'm looking for help.' The sergeant-major was one who could keep a confidence. He outlined the story of the morning.

'That's serious,' Heather's voice said. 'You'll have to bring the police in.'

'I'm just about to pay them a visit. And it'll take up most of the day. They get more excited about attempted killings than we sometimes do. I suppose that follows from our different lines of business. But I intend to hold back what the girl let slip about the raid tonight. We don't want a lot of clumsy coppers frightening them off, do we?'

'No, Major, we do not.'

'I was thinking of a commando-style night exercise for a few volunteers. Some of those lads who helped out last time.'

'With respect, Sir, I don't think that Corporal Holly has the field experience for this one.'

'I agree,' Jonathan said. He was glad that the sergeant-major could not see the satisfaction which he was trying to keep out of his voice. 'I only used him last time because he looked young enough to pass for a student. Tonight, I was hoping that you could suggest an NCO or warrant officer with a little more experience and a lot of discretion.'

'I know just the man,' Heather said. The major could hear his smile. 'I'm doing nothing myself tonight.'

'That's fine. I don't know when I'll be free, so perhaps you'll take on the selection and preliminary briefing?'

They spoke for another ten minutes while Jonathan fed his change into the coin-box. When they were finished, he could be sure that no detail would be

overlooked in his absence. 'One more thing,' he added.
'Shona puked all over the car. I had to leave it in Nicol
Lane, off Broad Street. I'm hoping that the police
will finish with it quickly. There's a set of keys in a
magnetic box behind the back bumper and I left a fiver
under the driver's seat. Could somebody from the motor
pool . . . ?'

'Just you leave it to me, Major,' Sergeant-Major
Heather said comfortably.

'Make sure you warn him not to eat any peppermints
he finds lying around. Unless it's somebody you can do
without.'

Walking towards the police station, Jonathan passed a
church. There was a poster on the board outside.
'VENGEANCE IS MINE SAITH THE LORD', it
read.

Jonathan looked up at the sky. 'It's all right,' he said
aloud. 'You can have it back when I've finished with it.'

Police forces are geared towards saving the time of their
officers, not to avoiding delays and inconvenience to
victims and witnesses. It was already dark and uncomfortably late when, after perhaps an hour totalled in
making statements and answering questions but many
hours accumulated in just plain waiting, Major
Craythorne was at last free to go.

He took a taxi out to the barracks, changed his clothes
and collected his car, now smelling strongly of disinfec-
tant. Sergeant-Major Heather and his miniature task
force were already on their way. Jonathan phoned the
vet for news, got none and set off in pursuit of his men.

He drove to Dr Whelks's home. The doctor occupied
a substantial old house, hemmed on three sides by
fields. It was the only dwelling near the factory. As
Jonathan arrived the doctor emerged, followed by the
deep bark of at least one large dog, and showed him

where to leave his car. The doctor was already dressed, as Jonathan had advised him, in dark, warm, casual clothing.

They set off together with hardly a word necessary, crossed the unlit main road and climbed over a fence to enter the industrial estate by way of a strip of long-established trees. The night was cold and the trees moved gently in a chilling wind, but a thin rind of moon took the edge off the darkness. The doctor led them to the agreed rendezvous in a small copse near a corner of the factory.

Sergeant-Major Heather was in wait, and men were already arriving. They had been dropped at intervals a few miles off and told to make their way individually without being seen by a soul. Faces blackened, they loomed out of the dark, squatted and melted into the darkness again.

The sergeant-major accepted a key from the doctor. He counted heads. 'That's the lot, Sir,' he said.

'Listen carefully,' the major said. 'As far as you're concerned this is a training exercise, and if it should happen that certain people – who may or may not be the group who blinded my sister and poisoned my dog – blunder into it while acting illegally, well, that will be their bad luck.

'Our role is mainly to watch and to intervene only if necessary. We may have to gather up a sentry or a decoy. But the general plan is to let them trap themselves where they shouldn't be and where the police can round them up. So, no violence, or only the absolute minimum necessary for carrying out my orders.

'I have a gentleman with me who represents the factory. No names, etc. We'll call him . . . Nimrod, for present purposes. For the moment, I'll hand you over to him.'

Dr Whelks assumed a placatory expression although it is doubtful whether anybody could see it. 'Good evening,' he said. 'It happened that Major Craythorne's call this morning came at a time when the laboratories had nothing very urgent or contentious going on. So the rest of the day was spent setting the scene.' He took several minutes to explain the geography of the building and the routes by which the laboratories might be reached.

'The animal-houses have been cleared,' he went on, 'and so have the small laboratories and the big lab. Everything expensive, important or confidential has been moved to store. I don't think our friends will find anything to interest them until they've passed through the big lab to the special lab beyond. That's a secure space, only used when the work in hand is dangerous or a commercial secret, or occasionally as overflow. It is also rodent-proof. All the cages of rodents have been moved in there, and we've set up some scrap glassware to simulate the kind of experimental work which these people probably imagine us doing. They can break the glass if it gives them any satisfaction, and it won't matter a damn if they open the cages.'

'Nimrod and I,' Jonathan said, 'will remain here, which is HQ. You chaps will shadow any visitors, invisibly if you can, and keep us informed by radio, getting well out of earshot before going on the air. Got it?'

'What will the factory guards be doing?' a voice asked.

'One man will patrol as usual while his partner mans the gatehouse,' said Whelks. 'As far as either of them is concerned, you lot are invisible. So also are any visitors until I say otherwise.'

There were no more questions.

CSM Heather breathed a word of command which

made the men jump. He led them away to their positions, returning twenty minutes later to report that all was ready. The sergeant-major had a tactician's eye for ground and Jonathan was happy to leave the disposal of the men to him.

They waited with the patience which is learned only by soldiers and tarts. Dr Whelks, who had not had the benefit of training in either profession, was inclined to fret. Jonathan, now that he had resumed smoking, felt the desperate need of a cigarette.

Exactly at midnight, their patience was rewarded. 'Sir,' whispered a voice. 'Dobson, Sir.'

'Watching the gate,' said Heather, aside. 'Go on, lad.'

'Both the guards are at the gatehouse. A car just stopped under the lights and a lady got out. Very large and respectable, both of them. She seems to be asking the guards to help her. Yes, they're lifting the bonnet.'

'We're off,' said the major.

'Hetheridge here, Sir,' said the radio.

'Overlooking Entry B,' said the CSM. Entry B was by way of a ditch which ran from a culvert under the road and passed within a hundred yards of the factory. 'Go on, Hetheridge.'

'Three people moving up the ditch. Two men and a girl, looks like.'

'How could he tell them apart in this light?' Jonathan asked the sergeant-major. 'Mating instinct?'

'I put him there because he's got the best night vision of the lot,' Heather said.

'Ah. Make sure they haven't left a sentry,' Jonathan said into the radio. 'Then follow, but stay well back. Sands can pick them up from the roof of the solvent store. Got that, Sands?'

'Got it, Sarn't-Major. Hang on a mo'.'

'Time we gave them another course on proper radio procedures, Sir,' Heather said.

'Yes, but some other time,' Jonathan said.

'Another one coming up the ditch,' said Hetheridge's voice. 'A man. And there's another girl heading cross-country to meet them. They're having a bit of a confabulation in among some bushes. Shall I try to get close?'

'Definitely no,' Jonathan said. 'Stay well back and wait.'

'I got 'em,' said Sands's voice suddenly. 'They're out of the ditch an' pussyfooting across the bit o' lawn to the canteen windows. Looks like they're planning to break in. Yerse, I see now. The old treacle-and-brown-paper trick. How original can you get?'

'I always said that Sands knew too much for his own good,' Jonathan whispered. 'Nimrod, do we let them break a window?'

'Yes. Of course. Cheap at the price.'

'Who's in the shrubs by the main doors?' Jonathan asked Heather.

'Higgs and Sanderson. Higgs has the radio.'

'Right.' Jonathan pressed the Transmit button. 'Higgs.'

'Sir.'

'They're going in through the canteen. Use the key, pick them up in the concourse and follow. Don't alarm them.'

'Sir.'

'Major, Sir,' said another voice.

'Yes, Sands.'

'Four've gone in, but one of them stayed outside, guarding their retreat.'

'Keep an eye on him. We may want you to gather him in later.'

'He's moved round the corner to the front of the building. I think he's got an aerosol, Sir. Probably intends to fill in the time with a little signwriting.'

'Stop him,' Whelks whispered to Jonathan.

'Sands,' Jonathan said. 'Nimrod doesn't want graffiti. You and . . .'

'Crispin,' said the sergeant-major.

'You and Crispin grab the sentry now. Whatever else, don't let him give the alarm. Dobson?'

'Sir.'

'There may be some kerfuffle at the front of the building. If the decoy takes fright, grab her. No hurry. The gatemen should have the sense to keep the car immobilised.'

'I'll leave the outside in your hands,' Dr Whelks said. 'I'm going in, to catch up with your chap Higgs.'

'I'll tell him,' said Jonathan. 'You can contact me on his radio.'

Several minutes passed in radio silence. Jonathan flexed his muscles for warmth in the cold stillness. Suddenly, silence was gone.

Fifty yards away, feet pounded on tarmac. 'Bugger's bolted,' Sands's voice said over the radio. Sergeant-Major Heather drew in his breath in a hiss which boded ill for Sands's tranquillity over the next few days.

'Catch him,' Jonathan said. 'Or, if he's too quick for you, at least make sure he doesn't double back.'

Heather took the microphone back from his major. 'And if he's too quick, you'll both be on cross-country running for the next fortnight,' he said.

The radio fell silent. The sound of footsteps had died away.

'Sir, Dobson,' said the radio. 'The decoy's getting the wind up. Voice going shrill and arms waving. Wants the gatemen to get her car going right away, but they've got half the wiring out. I reckon she heard the fuss and she's beginning to wet herself.'

'Grab her, gently, if she tries to run for it. Otherwise hang on.'

99

Ten minutes crawled away into limbo. Then Dr Whelks's voice came over the radio, with the precision of thought and timing of one more used to dictating into a tape-recorder. 'Nimrod here. Are you there, Major?'

'Go ahead, Nimrod.'

'All is secure in here. Please have your men bring in the decoy and the sentry.'

'The sentry took fright,' Jonathan said. 'My men haven't caught him yet.'

'The decoy, then. Bring him· or her to me, in silence. Go in through the front doors, across the concourse into the corridor beyond, first right and continue straight ahead to the big lab. There is a door at the far end of the lab. The key will be in the outside. Put him in there with the others. I shall stay out of sight until it is done. Then your men will withdraw. I propose to keep the radio for the moment. You remain on guard in case the sentry returns. Is that all right?'

'Understood. Will do,' Jonathan said. 'Dobson, you got that?'

'Got it, Sir. We're moving now.'

The radio went silent and then came alive again. All that came over was the sound of heavy breathing. For a moment Jonathan expected an obscene radio-message. Then he understood. 'What is it, Sands?'

'This is Allbright, Sir,' said a hoarse voice with a strong Liverpool accent. 'Sands is knackered. The . . . the sentry got away from us. There was a car backed into a lane, half a mile along the road. Drove off like the clappers, Sir. Worst driving I ever did see. I don't reckon he's coming back.'

'I don't either,' Jonathan said, 'but stay on watch. What kind of car was it?'

'Looked like a small Ford, from the shape. Maybe an Escort or one of the Japanese copies, Sir. Couldn't see the colour.'

'Too bad,' Jonathan said mildly. 'Was anybody waiting at the car?'

'Definitely not, Sir. If he'd fumbled much longer with the keys, we'd have caught him.'

'That seems to be the active part of the night over,' Jonathan said to Heather. 'I think we could smoke now.'

Two hours and seven cigarettes later, Dr Whelks came back on the air. He sounded pleased with himself. 'Major Craythorne? I shall be phoning the police and the press in a few minutes. You and your men withdraw now. I'll return your radio to you at the barracks this evening and bring you up to date.'

'I'm relieved,' Jonathan said. 'I thought that you might intend to keep them for human guinea-pigs. Is the subject of my Photo-fit with you? If so, I'm coming in.'

'Nobody resembling it. Not unless he's shrunk several inches and grown a pair of ears that remind me of a wing-nut. Your man will have been the sentry.'

Jonathan Craythorne used a word which he had picked up from the men. If the man who had poisoned his dog had slipped through the net, he had wasted a lot of army time and risked his colonel's wrath for nothing.

THIRTEEN

Inspector Cheyne was a wily old hand at the interrogation of witnesses. Knowing this, the colleagues in whose area the fur farm belonged had invited him to have first crack at the night's haul.

The Wendocks had decided that a total silence was the best defence. The other detainees were in their various ways more forthcoming. Mrs Colcarth had demanded her solicitor and had refused to be silenced until she got him. Terry Janson had resorted to mere abuse.

So Cheyne was concentrating on Eric Foulkes, the only one of the five prisoners too demoralised in the face of imminent disgrace to comprehend his rights when given the usual caution.

'I think you're in serious trouble,' Cheyne said at one point. 'Your own mother wouldn't believe that story. It's the worst I've ever heard.'

'It's the truth,' Eric insisted for the third or possibly the fourth time. He had lost count.

'Truth or not, I can see a court falling about with laughter. And that,' the inspector added, 'may well be your best line of defence. I've known a court go easier on a defendant who gave them a good laugh.'

'The others will tell you exactly the same.'

'I doubt it. Even so, you had plenty of time to get together and agree a story after the watchmen locked you inside and sent for us. The press, of course, are muzzled until the case comes on. But they've already got the story and photographs. After your conviction they'll be free to spread themselves. And then you'll look a real bunch of Charlies. Won't you?'

Eric buried his face in his hands. It was answer enough. He also muttered something inaudible.

'Speak up,' said the inspector. 'My constable can't hear you.'

Eric opened his hands slightly. 'It can't be that serious,' he said. 'We broke into the factory, to protest against vivisection. All right, big deal, we'll take our medicine. None of the rest of it happened the way it looks, but if it had happened it still wouldn't have been criminal.'

The inspector decided that it was the time to shift his ground. 'Possibly true,' he said. 'But there's a far more serious matter. Murder. At Ridgeback Fur Farm.'

Eric raised his face again. It was stained with tears. 'I don't know what you're talking about,' he said.

'Pull the other one. We've found mink-fur on your clothes. You must consort with a very well-dressed lady? Or do you have your own mink coat?'

'Some of my patients have fur coats,' Eric said.

'Give us their names and we'll have the fur compared under a microscope. But I wouldn't advise you to bank on the result. You were a fool to wear the same shoes again last night, shoes with heavy cleats and a distinctive pattern of wear. The footprints in the mud at the fur farm were as sharp as I've seen. The pattern of the soles matches exactly. And, just in case you think of claiming that somebody borrowed your shoes, we can prove that you were wearing them. Length of stride, angle of foot, distribution of weight, the lot. Why did you think we led you along a muddy path when we brought you in?'

'But that . . .' Eric fought to pull himself together. 'Even if I'd been at the fur farm,' he said, 'which I'm not admitting, that wouldn't mean that I'd done anything worse than release a few mink to draw attention to their plight, and paint some slogans on the walls. And the man had a heart attack. The papers said so.'

'The papers weren't present at the autopsy. Some mink were released,' the inspector admitted. 'More than seven hundred went missing. But the local keepers tell me that there's no indication that anything like that number ever saw freedom. A few dozen, just to camouflage the real objective which was the theft of pelts. Some stolen, un-numbered pelts were found in the possession of one of the smaller dealers. He might have got away with it if he hadn't tried to sell the skinned bodies to a maker of tinned dog-food. And the fur farm manager's prepared to swear that those pelts stem from his individual breeding. We've had a look at your bank-books. Business not been too good lately?'

'But that doesn't – wouldn't make it murder.'

'The pathologist is prepared to state that there was a blow struck under the man's ribs, and the rupture of the heart valves followed as a result. A felony was being committed at the time. That virtually rules out a plea of manslaughter. Your footprints were on the spot. And you once enrolled in a karate class.'

'All right,' Eric said desperately. 'All right. I'd been there. Money's tight and the Building Society's gunning for me. So we went after some mink-pelts. We didn't skin them, we just knocked them on the head and sold them like that.

'But I never hit anybody. The man appeared suddenly and came after us. I . . . I don't have the guts for a fight and, anyway, I'm past the age for rough-housing. I ran for it. I must have run past the place just a few moments before it happened. But I never even knew that a blow had been struck. It was . . . the other man, if anybody.'

'But you're the one we've got,' the inspector pointed out cheerfully. 'None of your friends from last night could have made the other set of footprints. And – ' The inspector gave the constable a meaning look and thereby missed Eric's change of expression. The constable raised his pencil and made scribbling motions just clear of the paper. ' – there's nothing to say that you didn't strike the blow. The footprints at the scene of the fight are too smeared by the violence of the action. Personally, I'm inclined to believe you. But if we don't get our hands on your friend, you're going to carry the can.' He nodded again to the constable, who resumed taking notes.

'Oh my God!' Eric wailed. 'It was Mike. Mike Underhill. But he swore to me afterwards that he'd never laid a hand on this man.'

The inspector concealed his satisfaction. It was not only a name, Underhill. It was a label. And it was a signpost pointing to a wanted man. Just one word. Underhill.

'While we're on the subject of Mike Underhill,' he said, 'let's go back a bit, to the affair of the chemists' shops which resulted in the blinding of the lady customer. . . .'

FOURTEEN

In the Mess there was a small Visitors' Bar which, except on Guest Nights, was as far as the civilian was usually allowed to penetrate into an area where the officers of the regiment preferred to talk shop without concern over the Official Secrets Act. It was a small, stark room with little pretension to the comparative comfort which could be found in the Mess proper, but it served its purpose.

Major Craythorne furnished Dr Whelks and himself with a whisky apiece, signed the book and accepted the return of his radio from the doctor. They settled at a table in the empty room.

'You'd better set my mind at rest,' Jonathan said. 'The town's buzzing with rumours.'

The doctor looked amused. 'Like what?' he said.

'Oh, rumours which, taken together and reconciled, suggest that your visitors wrecked a lot of experimental work, released about ten thousand rats and mice, and were later found drunk and naked enjoying some kind of orgy. At least, it's generally assumed that they must have been enjoying it. Exaggerated, of course . . .'

Dr Whelks slowly shook his head.

'Not exaggerated? My, my! Rumour also has it that, when first apprehended, the villains produced a story to which nobody is inclined to give credence. A story which includes military or paramilitary gentlemen with blackened faces who frogmarched a hitherto respectable lady into the building, and a tall figure in a white coat and surgical mask who spun them tales of contact with some horrible disease, the Latin name of which they were unable to recall, thereby persuading them to remove their clothing for decontamination. The fact that their clothes were found scattered around the outer lab doesn't seem to have helped their credibility.'

'Not a lot,' Whelks agreed.

'Rumour also has it that they tried to explain their drunkenness by stating that the same white-clad gentleman – who seems remarkably akin to the mad scientist beloved of fiction – administered what he said were prophylactic injections but which may have been pure vodka. An almost-empty vodka-bottle is said to have been found – again, in the outer lab.'

'For once,' said the doctor, 'rumour seems to have approximated very closely to the truth.'

'Your visitors seem to have been very careless, or very gullible,' Jonathan said. His initial laughter had died on him.

'An hour in the dark, with thousands of rats and mice loose around them, had lowered their morale more than somewhat.'

'In the dark? It would certainly have lowered mine,' Jonathan said with a slight shudder. 'That was a bit harsh, wasn't it?'

Whelks shrugged. 'It was necessary. The modern, white laboratory rat – the Wistar – is a rather nice little chap. Under bright light, it would take a neurotic, or at least somebody sensitive to the point of folly, to be afraid of him. Rustling around in large numbers in the dark, of course, is something different. After an hour alone with the scuttling sounds and their own imaginations, our visitors would have believed anything. I could have sold them on the Second Coming, had I felt so inclined.

'They handed me out their clothing like lambs, and I flung it around the outer lab with, I must admit, some gusto. The old dame's silk drawers I draped over a fume-cupboard as if cast there in reckless abandon. And, when I explained that I did not propose to enter the chamber and be contaminated along with them, they presented their bottoms obediently to the door – which I wedged in a slightly-open position.' Whelks stopped and looked at Jonathan. 'You look concerned.'

'Do I? I suppose I am. They had it coming to them, but ... did you have to disgrace them quite so completely?' he asked.

'Perhaps not. But I've taken quite a lot from these people over the years. I thought,' Whelks said sadly, 'that you might have enjoyed their discomfiture. You, after all, have also suffered at their hands.'

'I would probably have given three hearty cheers if that man, Mike, had been caught along with them. Perhaps illogically, I blame him alone for my sister's blindness. He then seems to have tried to poison me and got my dog instead.'

'I take your point,' Whelks said. 'And I meant to ask after the patient.'

'Shona? Hanging on.'

'Helped, no doubt, by some of my firm's veterinary products. Had you thought of that? Well, it's hardly my fault that your chaps let your personal quarry bolt for it,' Whelks pointed out.

'True,' Jonathan said. 'But I must admit to a sneaking sympathy for the rest of them. I think they're misguided. I think they get reformers a bad name as cranks. But I do believe that they're sincere and that there is something worth being sincere about.'

'Go on,' said the doctor. 'You interest me. You're not thinking of joining their ranks?'

'Not that, no.' Jonathan fumbled for words. He was stumbling through unfamiliar territory. 'I've been doing some reading and some listening, since you gave me the guided tour,' he said. 'And I think that the law is crazy and outdated. It permits experiments to be repeated for the advancement of individuals' careers, or carried out in search of knowledge with no foreseeable application. But, worst, it requires new products to be tested to a standardised pattern which is almost a recipe for suffering.'

'Ah,' Whelks said. 'The RD Fifty test of ill-repute, now phasing out. Hit-or-miss experimentation to find the dosage which kills half the subjects in fourteen days. That does use up far more than the minimal number of animals. And products of low toxicity must kill in that time by sheer volume rather than by poisoning. But I'm afraid that it's the only kind of test producing a simple classification of toxicity which the bureaucratic mind can understand. I'll add something which you probably don't know. The EEC has worsened the situation, by requiring the classification of all products in transit.'

'On top of which,' Jonathan said, 'there must be an enormous amount of product-testing when the law doesn't require it, just to be able to show that every care was taken in the event of some unforeseen effect. It all adds up to numbers of animals beyond my comprehension, most of them being killed unpleasantly and perhaps unnecessarily. Or am I wrong?'

Dr Whelks sat silent for some time before he spoke. 'No,' he said. 'You're not wrong. Over-simplifying a bit, perhaps. But I agree with what you say.'

'Well, then—'

'I hadn't intended to explain, not at this stage. But since you've raised the questions, I'll tell you some more. In strictest confidence for the moment.'

'Hang on,' Jonathan said. 'I'll top us up again.' He went to the hatch and rang for the barman. He was not too sure that he wanted to know any more, but he had gone too far to turn back. He lit another cigarette while he waited for service. Now he was going to have to stop all over again. But not just yet.

When they were settled with fresh drinks, Dr Whelks

went on. 'I've been concerned for years over mass testing on animals. No sensible person could become involved in this line of work and not have his qualms.

'And yet, up to now, what was the alternative? Let's say that you were to fall seriously ill tomorrow. Would you willingly be the first patient to use a new promising drug if it had not been tested first – on animals or by some other method no less effective?'

'I don't suppose I would,' Jonathan said.

'You're damn right you wouldn't. But one trouble is that our legislation is almost unaltered since eighteen seventy-six. That was more than a hundred years ago. Another problem is that animal tissues don't always react as human tissue does. Thalidomide was subject to searching tests on animals. Some doubt has been thrown on the integrity of the tests, but the fact seems to remain that the drug has little effect on animal embryos. Conversely, if aspirin had been subject to the same tests it would never have been adopted. It kills most rodents.

'In recent years, other possibilities have arisen. It's now possible to culture human cells or tissues from small original samples, with two prime advantages. Firstly that they are in fact human and behave as such. And secondly that they can be kept uncontaminated.

'I've been working on this line for years, in co-operation with other, similar labs, and for the last two years I've been chairing an international committee. We now have tissues in culture from every human and embryo organ. It is possible to establish a testing system almost independent of animals and more reliable. We can go into mass production for all medical and pharmaceutical testing, at any time that law and public opinion will allow.

'But those two forces have enormous inertia. And there are those whose interests lie the other way. Breeders of animals for laboratory purposes, for instance.

'We're ready now to make public announcements and to start lobbying the legislatures of the participating countries. But, in the normal course of things, change might take another hundred years. Or it might happen tomorrow, given a surge of publicity and public sympathy.'

Jonathan sat up suddenly and pointed a finger at the doctor. 'So that's it! You sacrificed those poor, misguided sods on the altar of publicity.'

'I'm afraid that's the truth,' Whelks said. 'We'd rather have had the other sort of publicity. But this will reach the public consciousness all right. It has everything from cuddly bunnies to orgies. The media will want to fill in the background, and the rest will follow. I'm booked to speak on television over the next few months, and this will focus the attention we desperately need. It will give us a springboard.

'It's ironic. The aims of these people will be achieved. They've argued for years that we should use human volunteer guinea-pigs, although if you asked one of them to volunteer he'd run a three-minute mile. Then they switched their argument to *in vitro* testing before the world, or science, was ready for it. Now, four of them will be sacrificed to ridicule and punishment in order to achieve their very goals, and they'll never even know it.'

They fell silent again.

'There's a sort of poetic justice,' Jonathan admitted at last. 'Or there would be if they'd caught the man Mike.'

'They'll get him,' the doctor said. 'I saw the police again just before I came here. They've got his other name now, and they hinted that they're after him for something more serious even than the attempt on your life.'

They fell silent again. Jonathan offered another drink,

111

but the doctor said that he was driving.

'There'll be just as much objection to using cultures of human tissues,' Jonathan said suddenly.

'I expect so.'

'Embryo tissues. That smacks of experimenting on unborn babies. The public will scream.'

'Possibly,' the doctor said. 'But they could save their breath. You only need a few cells to start with and you can go on proliferating for ever. I provided the original stock. Not long ago, my wife had a miscarriage, alive but too early to be viable. It appears that she can't carry full-time. I did the necessary work myself. And I'm quite prepared to tell the world.'

'I'm sorry,' Jonathan said.

'Don't be.' The doctor managed to produce a twisted smile. 'If I can't leave a human inheritance behind me – and only vanity suggests that I should – then I'm happy to think of embryonic organ-tissue cultures of the future, doing work of fantastic usefulness, averting infinite animal suffering, and all descended from myself. My name will be perpetuated in the name of the cultures and may be alive long after my progeny would have died out.'

'But wouldn't you rather have had a child?' Jonathan asked before he could stop himself.'

For a few moments the doctor stared through the fibreboard walls to some scene which only he could visualise. Then he gave himself a small shake. 'To judge from the experiences of our friends,' he said, 'we'll be better off sticking to Labradors.'

FIFTEEN

Jonathan excused himself from dining in the Mess. Instead, he ate a hasty snack and drove into the town to visit the sick.

The vet was just finishing evening surgery and took time off to conduct him through to the back premises. Several pets were recovering from anaesthesia, and in a small, separate room Shona lay on a clean palliasse. Her lean frame was skin and bone. The beautiful, russet coat was thin and dull and her eyeballs were yellow with jaundice. A bottle dripped gently into her foreleg. Despite her state she was conscious and she managed a small movement of her tail when they entered.

'You can see how it is,' the vet said in an undertaker's voice. He hated having to break bad news. 'She's holding her own or even making slight progress. She's getting enough nourishment to sustain life. But the longer her organs are out of use the slower her recovery will be. Frankly, if she doesn't eat soon I'm not sure that she'll ever be her old self again.'

'I see,' Jonathan said huskily.

'We've tried, but she won't swallow. And putting a tube down her throat while she herself doesn't believe that her insides are ready for food would do more harm, emotionally, than the food would do physical good. She might take it from you. Would you like to try?'

'Yes, of course.'

The vet went away and returned with a bowl of what seemed to be warm custard. 'I've added a mild analgesic and something to take down the inflammation,' he said. 'It'll do nothing but good. Coax her if you can. I'll come back later and see how you're getting on.'

Jonathan settled down to his task. Shona seemed to

take comfort from his voice. After a little coaxing, she would accept the spoon in her mouth. But swallowing seemed to be beyond her. Again and again the mixture dripped out of the side of her mouth onto a paper which the vet had spread beneath her head.

Jonathan ran out of comforting words. But when his voice stopped, Shona seemed to lose interest. For lack of anything else to say, he started to tell her about the events of the past thirty-odd hours. It helped him a little to sort the issues into words. He knew that she could not understand, but at least she was responding to his voice. Once, she swallowed; but when he broke off she seemed to lose interest again. He resumed the story. Perhaps the soothing admixtures helped, but after a few minutes she accepted and swallowed another mouthful, and then another. Soon she was trying to gulp.

The story and the bowl were finished together. Shona relaxed. Jonathan sat with his fingers stroking what remained of her coat. When he fell still, she groaned in discontent.

'You're right,' Jonathan said. He gave her one last, gentle pat. 'There's a missing element. The girl. One person ran off from the factory. There was nobody at the car. There should have been two of them. Where the hell has she got to? She seemed keen enough to go along with her pals while you were puking all over her. Not your fault,' he added quickly. He sat for another few moments and then bestirred himself. 'I'll have to run along now, old thing. I'll see you again tomorrow.'

He returned the empty bowl to the vet, who turned it upside down and looked pleased. 'She didn't throw any of it up again?'

'Not so far.'

The vet's face broke into a grin. 'In about a fortnight's time, you'll have a dog again,' he said.

SIXTEEN

Although Inspector Cheyne had had a day which went far towards reducing his backlog of unsolved cases, it had been a long day. He was very much looking forward to going home for a stiff gin, a meal, a hot bath and a good night's sleep when Major Craythorne's name reached him from the desk.

He was tempted to refuse on the grounds that he was already off duty. But the major had been helpful in the past and would probably be one of his best witnesses in the future. Moreover, this need take only a minute.

He met Jonathan in the same bleak interview room. 'If you've come for news,' he said, 'I can tell you that we've made four arrests and expect to make another soon.'

'The other one being the man called Mike?' Jonathan asked.

'Correct. We now know his surname,' the inspector said rapidly and without sitting down, 'and we've identified him. We've even visited his flat. Substances removed for forensic examination should go a long way towards obtaining convictions in the cases of tampering with the contact-lens solutions, attempting to poison yourself and another charge which I can't disclose for the moment. Two sets of fingerprints in the flat were repeated on that pair of tongs in your car. In another context, we were interested to learn that he has a half-brother in the SAS. And now, if that's all, I was just going home.'

Jonathan remained firmly in his chair. 'Have you found any sign of the girl?'

'Mary Jennings? No. There were signs that a woman had stayed in the flat, that's all. Why?'

'Because I'm worried,' Jonathan said. 'Yesterday, she acted along with Mike, under considerable pressure, in an attempt on my life. But when I interrupted them, she stood her ground and she certainly saved my dog by telling me what had happened and what poison had been used. She got into my car with me and we drove to the vet. She was in a state of mental confusion, torn between loyalty to her group, duty and, I'm quite sure, fear of the man Mike.

'Although she tried not to give anything away, she was in a position to betray Mike. And, in the circumstances, I certainly wasn't paying any attention to whether or not I was followed to the vet's surgery. If I'd been in Mike's shoes, I'd have followed.

'When I went inside, she stayed in my car. She promised to be there when I came out, but she wasn't.'

'So she panicked,' the inspector said.

'Possibly. But I can't help visualising something else. His car stopping near mine. The man getting out. He's very angry. His attempt on me has failed and I've got solid evidence against him. He thinks she's let him down. He wants to know what she told me. And, when she denies having betrayed him in any way, he doesn't believe her. You must know how such quarrels can flare up.'

Inspector Cheyne sat down slowly. 'Only too well,' he said. 'But we've come across no signs of violence. No bodies. Nobody admitted to hospital. Probably, they've gone off together. She'll turn up.'

Jonathan was remembering that only one person had slipped through the net at the factory, but he was hoping that the military presence on that occasion need never come out. 'Have you checked whether she returned home?' he asked.

'Yes. She hasn't. But what of that? Girls don't always go home. They wait until the parents have got over the shock of their little girls going off with a bloke. Then they phone home to find out whether all's forgiven.'

'So you haven't looked for her?'

'No,' Cheyne said impatiently. 'Why would we? She hasn't been reported as a missing person, and we've no evidence yet on which we could bring a charge against her. We'll find out more when we catch the man.'

'Is there any indication that Mike had another place where she could be hidden? Willingly or unwillingly?'

'None at all. You're barking up the wrong tree, Major.'

'Perhaps. But I can't rid myself of the picture of an angry man dragging a frightened girl out of my car and driving off. All right, maybe he drove her to the station and sent her off to stay with his auntie. Or maybe he killed her. Or ... My dog had sicked all over her clothes. Maybe she couldn't stand the stink any longer and went off to change and then didn't bother to contact me again. In any of those eventualities, only time will tell; and time would be unimportant.

'But suppose that he shut her in somewhere. It's been – what? – nearly thirty-six hours now since she was in my car. I think it's high time you looked for her.'

'But looked where?' the inspector asked reasonably. 'She isn't in his flat, that's been searched so thoroughly we couldn't have missed a hair. If he had use of a garage or workshop or shed, we don't know of it.'

Jonathan was beginning to feel that he was making a fool of himself, but that feeling had never bothered him. He persisted. 'Have you found his car?'

'Yes. Parked near the railway station. We towed it here. The forensic science lads will be going over it tomorrow.'

'Has the boot been opened?'

'Not yet. It was locked and we don't have the keys. There didn't seem to be any urgency, with its owner still on the loose.'

117

'We're both going to head for home shortly, Inspector,' Jonathan said. 'Let's just take a look on the way by, shall we?'

'If it'll get you off my back.'

The two men walked down to the police garage. A civilian employee, changing wheels on a police Range Rover, was the only occupant. The garage seemed to magnify the sound of traffic on the dual carriageway behind it.

Mike Underhill's Ford Escort crouched at the end of the garage, beside a workbench which was backed by racks of tools.

'Let's take a look in the boot,' Jonathan said.

'I'm afraid we can't. Look at it. It's been sealed.'

'Seals can be broken.'

'Not by me, they can't,' said the inspector. 'It's part of the procedure for preserving evidence. Any container is sealed and passes from hand to hand that way, under signature. If a seal gets broken, other than by the proper hand in the proper time and place, the evidential value is destroyed and heads roll. Somebody decided that the boot was a container which might contain evidence, so he sealed it pending the arrival of the forensic science team, and the fact is recorded.'

'Evidence be damned. It might contain a live girl,' Jonathan said.

'You've no reason to suppose so.'

'And you've no reason to suppose not.'

'No . . . Yes I do,' the inspector corrected himself. 'If your vision was the true story, they'd have removed the evidence from your car.'

'Not necessarily. The damage was already done. And in the heat of a quarrel . . .'

Inspector Cheyne stooped and put his ear to the boot. 'I can't hear anything,' he said. 'And there's no smell of dog-puke.'

118

'She could be unconscious. Or tied and gagged. You wouldn't hear much with that traffic going past.' As he spoke, Jonathan wondered whether Mary Jennings might not be listening helplessly to his words, waiting to know her fate. 'But suppose, just suppose, that your forensic chaps open the boot in the morning and they find Mary Jennings, freshly dead of suffocation or hypothermia. How will you look and feel?'

The inspector listened once more at the boot and then frowned at Jonathan. 'I'll have to think about this,' he said.

Jonathan remembered then that the inspector had shown himself to be capable of liberal thought. 'Why don't you think about it over there?' he asked.

The inspector nodded and walked to the further end of the garage.

Jonathan took a tyre-lever out of the rack and inserted it beside the lock. The boot-lid resisted and then sprang open.

Mike Underhill's corpse was curled in a foetal position in the cramped space, but his head was twisted so that his eyes, glazed with the desiccation which follows death, glared up at the ceiling. His teeth were bared in an unpleasant snarl. The horn-handle of the sheath-knife stood out from his chest.

Inspector Cheyne was content to accept responsibility for breaking the seal and opening the boot. As a virtual bystander, Jonathan was soon free to go.

Driving back to barracks, Jonathan was stopped by traffic-lights although the streets were empty. He halted, irritated at being delayed pointlessly by a mindless electronic signal. While he waited, he glanced around.

He knew the place well. It was on the route between his bank and his usual parking-place, by way of a park

119

where Shona liked to dally.

On the corner was a large building with few windows. Its occupancy was marked only by a small plate, inscribed 'G. & K. CONSULTING LABOR-ATORIES LTD', which Jonathan had never noticed. He only remembered that Shona had never liked to walk at heel near the building, and when he had once taken her past on the lead she had thrown back her head and howled.

The lights changed at last and he drove on.

SEVENTEEN

The Wendocks were at home, indulging in a fretful and unpromising discussion of their troubles, when their doorbell chimed. Since the disaster of their incarceration and capture at the factory, they had clung to each other for comfort. They went to the door together.

The student, Terry Janson, was on the step. His head was aligned with a distant street-lamp, which seemed to blaze redly through his ears.

Lucy was glad to recall a past indignity and so to release her temper. 'You!' she said. 'You've got a bloody nerve, coming here.'

'I suppose I have. All right,' Terry said, 'I was out of line, misled by the fact that you look as if you'd put it about a bit, and you clipped my ear and called me every name in the book and some that aren't. And I apologised. Now, can we forget it and talk about something more urgent? On the doorstep, if you insist. Or do you want blood?'

'You'd better come in,' Hugh said grudgingly. Lucy stood her ground for a moment and then moved aside.

Terry strolled through into the living-room, selected the most comfortable chair with a practised eye and dropped into it. The Wendocks took the settee and looked at him with dislike.

'So,' Hugh said at last. 'How come you're here?'

'I'm out on bail. Same as yourselves, I suppose.'

'That's not what I meant. Come to the point.'

'That is the point,' Terry said. There was a faint tremor in his voice, of fear or excitement, Lucy could not be sure. 'I've already got one fine hanging over me for breaking a court order. Now I've been caught again. I'm out on my own recognisances at the moment, but

121

by the time the magistrates have sat again I'll be needing bail. And if I'm still running around loose when the case is over I'll have another fine to pay, a thumper this time. I could use a smart lawyer, and they cost. I'm going to need money.'

'You won't get it from us,' Hugh said quickly. 'We've got to find money too. Try Mrs Colcarth. She landed us in this mess.'

'I've already been to see her. She doesn't want to know.'

'Well, then—'

'But we can get money,' Terry said. 'More than we need. You've heard about Mike?'

'Only what was in the Stop Press,' said Lucy. 'Isn't it terrible? What do you suppose happened?'

'It's obvious what happened,' Terry said.

'Mary?'

'If you think she could bring herself to harm him, and that she's strong enough to take his own knife away from him and kill him with it.'

'How do you know it was his own knife?' Hugh asked.

'It'd have to be, if Mary did it. The paper said "sheath-knife", and I can't see Mary with one of those on her belt. Right?'

Lucy's eyes came into sharp focus. 'But if it wasn't Mary, who was it?'

Terry's eyes locked with hers. He was no longer the frivolous and immature student they had known and despised. 'We know, don't we?' he said. 'You and I. Between us, we could prove it.'

Silence stretched while Lucy thought it out. Her sensual face showed no sign that, behind it, a keen mind was racing. 'I believe we could,' Lucy said slowly. 'But why . . . ?'

'Money.'

'From the mink farm?'

'You knew all about that, did you?'

'I guessed.'

'You're a clever girl,' Terry said. 'One tends to underestimate you, but there's no law says that sexy-looking birds can't have brains as well.'

Hugh was floundering a long way behind them. 'But who?' he asked plaintively. 'And why? I don't understand what you're talking about.'

'You don't have to,' his wife said. 'Just don't worry your head about it and I may be able to turn this disaster into a blessing. I'm going to phone and see if he's at home. You can mind the baby for an hour or two. Terry and I have business.'

They drove in silence for a while, each busy with dreams of sudden wealth. Terry spoke with a suddenness which made Lucy, at the wheel, jump. So that the Mini wavered perceptibly across the road. 'Would you have clunked me round the lug if I'd led up to it more gently?' he asked.

'Almost certainly,' she said. Her brassy exterior was invisible in the dark car, so that her gentle voice seemed to belong to a stranger.

'Almost?'

'With a ninety-nine per cent certainty,' she said. 'After all, I'm almost old enough to be your mother.'

'More almosts!' he said, laughing. 'Come off it. You're maybe six years older than I am. Seven at the most. As they say, by the time you're a hundred I'll be ninety-three. There's many a good relationship developed despite a far greater difference of ages.'

'Listen to the child!' she said. 'Wheelchair-snatching.'

He snorted with more laughter. 'There's a year or two yet before I'd have to push you around in a chair.'

She took time for a tricky venture through the traffic

before she replied. 'All the same, women do age more quickly. Another of life's sexist tricks.'

'If people have aged together, they don't see it,' he said. 'So my father told me. If we can get a good chunk of money out of this, what do you say? Let's take off together. I'll graduate in a few months. We could see the world.'

It was a temptation, she couldn't hide that from herself. He was young and vigorous and he had a devil-may-care attitude which Hugh would never have understood, let alone emulated. And he was older than his years. But she had ties. 'I have a baby,' she said.

'Bring it along or leave it behind, it's up to you.'

'It's not an it, it's a him.'

'Him, then.'

She thought of another objection. 'You couldn't travel around and get work as a designer.'

'I fancy working as a freelance photographer. That's travelling work.'

She could take this seriously, but was he joking? Or trying it on? 'Do you come on like this with all your fellow-students?' she asked.

'Them! Bloody infants. Either they're heading towards being blue-stockings without ever having lived, or they've not a thought in their little heads above having a good time while waiting for a husband who'd please Daddy. But you're different. You I could fancy. And you're a sticker.'

'You're asking me to unstick,' she pointed out.

'And I mean it. Hugh's all right, but he's not for a girl like you. You were made for adventure. I just know that you're the type who could throw your knickers over the windmill. The only question is whether you'd do so for me. What do you say?'

'I'll think about it.' She would, too, in the fastness of her half-sleeping fantasy-world. 'But, for now, we've

124

almost arrived. You'd better get your hand out of there,' she added, as if noticing the intrusion for the first time. The darkness hid her smile. She might or might not respond to his advances, but it was nice to have the option. Life was suddenly full of promise.

Lucy turned the Mini out of the street into a short, straight driveway with two lines of slabs set in gravel. At the far end was a small, concrete garage, squeezed uncomfortably between the house and the brick garden wall.

'He said to drive right in.'

'That makes sense,' Terry said. 'We don't want to be seen here either.'

Lucy drove into the garage. A clutter of gardening tools seemed to have been moved to the far end to make room for them. There was barely room to open the little car's doors.

Eric Foulkes met them outside the garage. He paused to pull down the steel door. 'No point letting everybody know our business,' he said. 'Come on inside.'

He led them into his fussy front room and pointed to chairs. 'You'll take a drink?' he asked.

'We're not here to be sociable,' Terry said.

'I think I'll have one,' said Eric. 'I don't usually drink when I've got patients coming, but I'm upset. About Mike.' The neck of the gin-bottle rang a small chime against the glass.

'I just bet you are,' Terry said. 'Committing murder can be very upsetting.'

'Whatever can you mean?'

'You know damn well what he means,' Lucy said. 'We've been talking about Mike's death and we can't see poor little Mary Jennings sticking a knife in him. Well, I mean, it'd have had to be when she got back to the car. Our raid on the factory had just gone wrong. They'd have been too busy to think about quarrelling.'

125

'And if they had quarrelled,' Terry said, 'I could believe Mike killing the girl, not the other way around.'

'I just don't believe this,' Eric said. 'We left Mike alive at the car. . . .'

'And,' said Lucy, 'some time between then and when Mary drove the car away, he was stabbed.'

'I was right behind you all the way,' Eric said. He blew his nose copiously into a large handkerchief and then hid his hands in his pockets where their shaking would not betray his fear.

'That's the whole point,' said Terry. 'You weren't. You were way behind and you only caught up just as we reached the factory.'

'So I stopped for a crap.'

'Try to convince the police of that when we point them in your direction. You think they'll find a human turd just where you said it would be?'

The doorbell whirred suddenly. Eric looked at the clock above the cold fireplace. 'That's a patient,' Eric said. 'Wait here. I won't be too long.'

They heard voices in the hall and then all was quiet. 'We've shaken him,' Lucy said. 'You think he'll cough up?'

'I don't know. He's a tricky little bugger. But we can do him more harm than he can do us and he knows it. I think I'll have that drink now. Just in case we don't get anything else off him. You?'

Lucy shook her head.

After twenty slow minutes they heard voices again and the slam of the front door. Eric returned and stood in the doorway. His face was mottled with a nervous rash and his nose was scarlet. 'What is it you're after? Your share of the mink money?'

'All of it,' Terry said. 'You tried to hold out on our shares. Now you can part with the lot, and serve you bloody right.'

126

'You've nothing to threaten me with,' Eric said with weak defiance. 'I haven't told them you were with us at the fur farm. Not yet. You were bloody lucky. That inspector let slip that they'd only found two sets of footprints which didn't belong. I was just going to drop you in it.'

'I didn't leave my great hoof-prints in the mud,' Terry said. 'They've already tried comparing my shoes, but I had the sense to stay on the concrete. Any story you tell now will sound like spite.'

'It's a hell of a lot of money, just to buy a little silence,' Eric said.

'That isn't all you get for the money,' Terry said. He winked at Lucy. 'Something happened on the way up the ditch. We were arguing about it. When Mary arrived, she asked you what was up and you didn't know. You'd better know the full story by the time they catch up with her or your head's on the block. That's what you're buying.'

Eric threw up his hands in defeat. 'The money isn't here,' he said. 'Come back again this time tomorrow night.'

The others exchanged a glance and a nod. 'Tomorrow night,' Lucy said.

Eric followed them out to the garage. Lucy's footsteps were almost dancing in triumph but Terry was worried. It had been too easy. There were twists which Eric could have tried. And he could easily have left his patient under the heat-lamp and crept out to the car. He made up his mind that they would drive a few yards up the road and then he would stop the car for a good going-over.

As they squeezed into the small car, Eric lingered outside the garage. So far so good, Terry thought. If there were a bomb under the car, Eric would have made himself scarce. Not that he would have had the skill or the materials for a bomb . . . Cutting the brake-pipes would be nearer his mark. Terry kept his hand near the parking-brake.

Lucy turned the key. The warm engine fired immediately and began to race. At the same moment, the steel door slammed down and Terry heard the sound of hammering.

'Stop the engine,' he said urgently. 'The bugger's trying to gas us with monoxide.'

Lucy turned back the key but the engine still raced. 'It doesn't work,' she said.

'Slam the car back through the door.'

She put the car into gear and reversed against the door, but it met a more solid resistance than an up-and-over garage door could provide. Already, Terry could feel his mouth drying with the build-up of carbon monoxide in the small space, but his mind still worked. 'Stall the engine,' he snapped.

'How-?'

It was quicker to do it himself. He managed to put his foot past the gear-lever while hauling up on the hand-brake. He kicked her foot away and trod on the clutch, pulled the gear-lever into top and lifted his foot again. The car leaped forward with a clatter of garden tools, but the engine stalled into blessed silence.

The atmosphere was choking. He knew that he would collapse in a moment and die soon after, but he still had the strength to get out of the car. The garage door was a snug fit and his efforts to shift it only increased his need for air. As his knees went and he rolled sideways, his last thought was that he might as well have stayed in the car and enjoyed a handful of Lucy.

But the demanding of money with menaces may well wear a gentle mask and does not always end in violence or bad blood.

On the morning following the ill-starred attempt by Terry Janson and Mrs Wendock to blackmail Eric Foulkes, Mrs Colcarth braved the world for the first time since the fiasco at the factory. The gatemen at Gillespie and Baker had made a less than perfect job of reassembling her Daimler and the car showed signs of resenting their casual treatment of its expensive workings.

At the garage in her nearest village, a smirking mechanic had promised to restore the car to good running order. But, he said, it would take until late afternoon.

Mrs Colcarth braced herself to walk the few miles home. She could feel the amused eyes of the villagers following her from every window, but she was a woman of courage and she could ignore their sniggering curiosity.

Less easily tolerated was the materialisation of several gentlemen of the press – a reporter and photographer from the local paper and another reporter from a national tabloid. They, along with others of their profession, had been refused interviews at her home but these individuals, more patient than the others or under stricter orders, had lingered in wait. Now they pounced, and Mrs Colcarth walked homeward with them snapping at her heels, asking embarrassing questions and refusing to accept evasions. The photographer held his camera ready to capture her first loss of temper.

To this dowager in distress there appeared a knight in dull, olive-green armour or, to be specific, Mr Morrow in his Land Rover. He stopped beside Mrs Colcarth and leaned over to open the passenger door, she climbed in and they were away, leaving the hounds to bay in vain.

'I can't thank you enough,' she said in a voice which was a pale shadow of its usual self.

'It was the least I could do,' he said with equal courtesy. 'You seemed hard-pressed.'

Mrs Colcarth summed up the press and its hounds in three short words. Mr Morrow was not shocked. He had often felt the same way.

When the Land Rover halted on the weedless gravel before Mrs Colcarth's front door, she was slow to get out. Mr Morrow's was the first sympathetic ear to attend her since the disaster. 'Why are you being so kind?' she asked.

'I'm always kind,' he said.

'I know. But after the way I spoke to you—'

'It's forgotten.'

'And all those things the papers have been saying!'

'I never believed one word of it,' he said.

'Won't you come in for a few minutes?' she suggested gratefully.

Morrow came inside. He refused alcohol but they shared a pot of tea and some dainty sandwiches. Mrs Colcarth found herself launched into a slightly expurgated version of the true story.

By the time she finished he was hiding a smile, because the tale, even as she told it, was irresistibly comic. But he managed to pat her hand consolingly.

'My solicitor doesn't expect a court to believe my story,' she said. 'But you believe me, don't you?'

He avoided the question. 'If the men on the gate won't back you up—'

'They've already denied it,' she said. 'And my car's been spluttering ever since they fiddled with it. That's why I've just taken it down to the garage. Do you think the mechanic could find proof that it was tampered with?'

Morrow felt that that was very unlikely. But at least he found the detail convincing. 'Yes, I believe you,' he said.

'Tell me honestly, what do you think my chances will be in court?'

He shrugged.

'I wouldn't mind being found guilty of raiding the factory,' she said. 'That would be quite . . . honourable. But the rest of it . . . If a court found that to be true, I couldn't bear the disgrace. I think I'd sell up and go abroad.' She dabbed her eyes with a miniature handkerchief edged in lace.

'I don't think that your friends have a leg to stand on,' Morrow said slowly. 'Your own case is different. Never mind your intentions. You claim that you were outside the gates and the gatemen were helping you with your car when you were virtually pounced on and dragged inside. The gatemen deny it, which makes your whole story suspect.'

'Then I may as well give up,' she said.

'Wait a minute. If you could prove the first part of your story – if, say, somebody driving past had seen and remembered your car and the men working on it – that would go a long way towards supporting your statement that you were taken inside against your will. It would be implicit that the gatemen hauled you inside, rightly or wrongly suspecting that you were a sentry for the group of invaders, and are lying to strengthen their own case.'

'I see that,' she said. 'But nobody came by.'

'You don't happen to remember, for instance, a Land Rover . . . ?'

Silence in the room was accentuated by the heavy ticking of the grandfather clock. She turned her plump wrist and gripped his hand. It was becoming clear to her that she had been pouring out most of her energy in support of the wrong cause.

'By the way,' she said at last, 'Mr Morrow, how much did you say it was going to cost us to restock the Wildfowl Park?'

131

EIGHTEEN

Jonathan enjoyed the town's riverside frontage. In summer, he found pleasure in walking Shona there, admiring the boats at their moorings, bright with paint and redolent of escape into another world. In winter, with the boats hauled ashore or laid up afloat all shrouded in tarpaulins and the water hurrying greyly towards the sea, he preferred to walk elsewhere.

But, only two days after the finding of Mike Underhill's body, some regimental trophies were due for collection from the silversmith who had been engraving them and whose shop fronted the river. Jonathan, glad of any excuse for a visit to his invalid setter, offered to fetch them.

Other duties took up his morning, but after lunch he drove into the city. The countryside was silvered with a rime of frost, but traffic had cleared the roads. He went first to the surgery.

Shona, mending fast, was off the drip and came to meet him, even managing a weak attempt at her old prance. If she maintained her progress, the vet said, she would be fit to leave by the end of the week.

Jonathan's singing voice had been likened to that of a tone-deaf crow but he hummed to himself when happy, and he was humming as he drove to pay an unheralded call at his sister's house.

There, his good mood was quickly spoiled. He found his sister's detestable sister-in-law, Agnes, not only present but at a loss to cope with Angela who, for the first time, had succumbed to self-pity.

'A donor turned up,' Agnes explained in a rapid whisper. 'A motorcycle accident. Severe head injuries, not expected to live. The parents had even signed the consent form. Then he made a miraculous recovery.'

Jonathan tried not to groan aloud. He could well imagine the conflicts which had been set up. He joined his sister on the living-room sofa and took her hand. She gripped it tight and turned her face to his shoulder.

'Another'll come along.' he said. 'Give it time.'

She had to struggle to speak through her tears. 'That's what's so awful,' she said. 'I was getting by all right, being very patient and virtuous. Then I thought that it was almost over. And now, there's a part of me can't help wishing that he'd died. Yet his death would have been worse than my having to stay like this a little longer. And all anybody can say is that there'll be another one, which makes me realise that what I'm hoping for is that somebody else will die or be killed.'

'It's a damnable position to be in,' he agreed. 'But your wishes won't make any difference to their chances of life or death. All you're really wishing is that when somebody runs out of luck you'll benefit, which will make their death a little less wasteful than it would have been. Can you remember that?'

'I'll try,' she said.

He would rather have faced an armed enemy than a woman in tears. He made his escape as soon as he decently could.

He was cursing the ill luck which had raised false hopes as he drove across one of the old bridges to park in front of the silversmith's shop.

Inside, he met with another check. The engraving was finished but the polishing would last another half-hour. He was offered a seat in the warm shop, but he preferred to wait in the car where he could divert his mind from his new trouble by listening to the radio, watching the light changing over the water and taking advantage of the respite to catch up with his thinking.

133

The newspapers had splashed the arrests of the ALF members, only to fall silent when formal charges were preferred and the facts became *sub judice*. Interest had revived with the finding of Mike Underhill. The disappearance of Mary Jennings was keeping it alive.

There had been no confirmed sighting of the girl since Jonathan had left her in his car three days earlier, although Jonathan suspected that she had been the lookout who had outrun his men at the factory. No good photographs of her had been found, so he had been pressed into compiling another Photo-fit portrait. This had appeared in the national press and on television. The customary understatement that its subject was required to help the police with their enquiries was negated by the news that the picture and description had been circulated to other police forces and to airports and docks.

Unlikely though it seemed, a lone girl without resources or worldly wisdom had vanished and left no trace whatever for the pursuers to find. Inspector Cheyne, in an unguarded moment, had expressed to Jonathan the opinion that she had run for London and had there fallen into the hands of the underworld. Probably, said the inspector, she was already at work in some expensive brothel.

Jonathan was not convinced. Mary Jennings was neither practised nor intelligent enough to travel without laying a trail. And his experience in Northern Ireland had taught him that, while a hunted man will move fast and try to outstrip his pursuers, a woman was more likely to go to ground immediately and completely, and would have the patience to stay there until all danger was past.

Idly, he wondered where he would look if he were in Inspector Cheyne's shoes. There was a caravan site not far away, deserted for the winter but with a dozen vans offering comfortable hiding to the fugitive. Or, still visible in the fading light, the laid-up boats on the old slipway across the street from him. Or, of course, the girl might know of some empty attic or cellar, somewhere where she had worked. She might even have a friend who had taken her in.

Jonathan's deliberations were interrupted when, from the corner of his eye, he saw the shop manager beckoning. He was humming again as he re-entered the shop. He knew where Mary Jennings was, to within a few feet. But he had no inclination to interfere, one way or the other. She had atoned for her share in earlier sins by standing her ground and giving Shona a chance of life. They were quits.

He signed the invoices and carried the two light cartons of silverware out to the car. He stowed them in the back, where Shona usually dwelt, and then sat down in the driver's seat and slammed his door.

'I thought I recognised your car,' said Mary Jennings in an unnaturally high voice. She was sitting, half-twisted, in the passenger's seat. As his eyes adjusted again to the near-darkness, he saw that she was holding a kitchen-knife, its point towards his ribs.

She was dressed, Jonathan noticed, in an assortment of sailor's gear – boots, jeans and an anorak – and she had given her hair a rough crop. There was also a faint smudge on her upper lip, suggesting a moustache. She could have passed for a delicately-built youth in the poor light. Her face looked drawn and he thought that there was a dangerous instability in her eye-movements and in the set of her mouth. He had noticed the same signs in a female IRA member as the net tightened, just before she triggered a grenade.

'Have you been getting enough to eat?' he heard himself ask.

The question took her aback. Her hand jerked and he felt the knife-point prick him below the ribs. 'I've done all right,' she said. 'Never mind that. What did you tell the police about me?'

It was vital that he gained her trust. He kept his hands on the wheel. 'I told them that you seemed terrified of Mike. I didn't tell them, and I don't propose to tell anyone, that you're living aboard *Dawn Chorus*.'

Again that jerk of the hand. The knife-point was dangerously intimate. He hoped very much that she would not be overtaken by a sudden sneeze. 'How did you know that that's where I was?'

'We're not far from the station, where Mike's car was found,' he explained calmly. 'I guessed that you might be on one of the boats. *Dawn Chorus* is the only one without any frost lying on the tarpaulin. I suppose you had to keep yourself warm.'

'There's a gas heater,' she said. 'I've been coming out at night for fish-and-chips and a discarded newspaper. Did you do that Photo-fit thing of me?' He was relieved to note that she sounded calmer.

'I had to. Anyway, they had photographs.'

'You made me look like a hag,' she said.

'I'm sorry.'

'It doesn't matter. Drive me away from here.'

'All right.' He started the car but delayed moving off. 'Where are we going?'

'You'll see. Go out past the army camp.'

Under the street lights he could, by calling on his unarmed combat training, have taken the knife away from her. But not without injury to one or both of them. Once they were on dark roads such a move would be too dangerous if not impossible. Yet he was intrigued enough to see it through. He drove off and circled onto the road which he would have taken back to barracks. Home-going traffic was heavy.

'Move the knife up a bit,' he said. 'I'd hate to be stabbed just because the car went over a pothole. If it's against my ribs you'll be less likely to shove it right in without meaning any harm.'

She lifted the knife a few inches. 'I can still do it if I want to,' she said.

'Of course. Do you mind if I smoke?'

'I could use one myself. Where are your fags? I'll light them. Or are you one of those macho pipe-men?'

'There are cigarettes and a lighter on the dash. Where my peppermints used to be. I can't seem to fancy a peppermint any more.'

'I don't suppose you can,' she said. She managed to light two cigarettes without taking the knife away. They smoked in taut silence while he picked his way through the traffic and out onto the emptier road. 'How's your dog?' she asked.

'Poorly, but on the mend.'

'That's all right, then,' she said. 'Your dog was the thing I've been most sorry about.' The tobacco seemed to have soothed her nerves. He could no longer feel the dangerous tremor through the knife-point.

'Weren't you a bit rash,' he said, 'to go on the raid with Mike dead in the boot of his own car?'

She astonished him by giving a hoot of half-hysterical laughter. 'You've got it all wrong,' she said. 'He wasn't dead then.'

'I'll be damned!' He thought it over while they swept past the guard-room of the barracks. The splash of lights around the main gates faded out of his mirror. 'I could have sworn that he'd gone for you while I was in the vet's surgery. When did . . . when did he die?'

'Never you mind.'

'At least tell me where we're going. I'm bound to find out that much, sooner or later.'

'We're going to collect some money which is due me.

It was due Mike, and he'd have wanted me to have it. I only had a few coins on me when it all went wrong, and Mike was always broke. I can't even afford another bag of chips, let alone get out of the country. You'll have to help. He won't part easily.'

'And then what? You drive off in my car, leaving me stranded in the wilds? And try to get out of the country without a passport?'

'I can't drive,' she said. 'Well, I'd had one lesson in Mike's car, but I wouldn't dare to try it on anything else. Especially not something big like this, with everything in different places.' She giggled suddenly, and he knew that her nerves were still over-stretched. 'I'll have to keep you on as my chauffeur.'

'Delighted to be of service.' He was thinking furiously. She had turned all his ideas upside down.

'You'll have to drive me to one of the Channel ports,' she said. 'I can go out on a return day-trip.'

'They've stopped letting you do that without a passport,' he said, without any idea whether it was true or not.

'I'll think of something. With money, I can lie low until I'm forgotten.'

She refused to say any more except to give him directions, and he let the miles go by in a silence broken only by the hum of the car.

They came to a halt at last outside one neat bungalow among a row, not far from the Gillespie and Baker factory. Jonathan leaned back as the girl peered past him.

'No lights!' she said. 'But he's got to be in. He's just got to! The paper said that he was out on bail.'

'That doesn't mean that he's at home all the time,' Jonathan said gently.

'No. We'll wait, that's what we'll do. There's nothing else. Nowhere to go, now that you know my hideout.'

She finished on a sob.

'You could always kill me, too,' Jonathan said. Testing the water, he thought.

'Don't be silly.'

'I could lend you some money,' he suggested. 'I've only a few quid on me, but we could drive to a bank where there's a cash machine.'

'Peanuts! I couldn't hide for long on what you could lend me,' she said. 'Mike was due seven and a half thousand, and that bastard collected the money but he wouldn't pay him. Wouldn't meet him alone or even speak on the phone. That's really why Mike was so uptight. If he'd had his share of the money, he could have skipped out and never mind if you'd been able to identify him. But thanks for the offer, if you meant it.'

'I meant it,' he said. 'But I'm damned if I know why.'

'You're not a bad sort of bugger, in spite of what Mike called you,' she said. 'Just a sweet, old-fashioned thing, comforting damsels in distress.' She twisted round to look at the road behind them. 'If he sees us here when he comes home, he'll scarper again. I know a place where we can wait. Drive on.'

He drove. They made two turns. He could tell that they were nearing the factory. Suddenly there was a group of bright lights beside the road and a police car parked nearby. She ducked her head as they went past.

Dr Whelks's windows were bright. The walls returned the sound of the engine to them.

They went on, and she said nothing.

'Where, then?' he asked.

'You'd better stop here,' she said dully. 'Anywhere you like. There's nowhere to go. Wherever I turn, they're there.'

He remembered a side-road from his perusal of the map three nights earlier. He found it, turned in and parked. The place was very dark. He left his sidelights on so that the interior would still receive some light from the instruments.

As near as he could guess, the police car and the bright lamps had been where the car had been waiting on the night of the raid. 'Was that the place?' he asked.

'Place?'

'Where you killed Mike.'

'I didn't kill him,' she said. 'But nobody'll ever believe me.' She put her head down on her knees. He could feel her sobbing. The whole car shook with it. He wondered where she had the knife.

NINETEEN

While Jonathan was visiting Shona, Eric Foulkes was confronting Inspector Cheyne. The same impersonal interview room, similar nagging, probing questions.

'I want to know why you've brought me back in here,' Eric said. He had meant to sound firm but he sounded petulant.

'Have patience a little longer,' said Inspector Cheyne.

'I've been patient. Very patient. But I was brought back in here last night and then I seemed to be forgotten.'

'Believe me, you were not forgotten,' Cheyne said. 'Far from it. But I found that there were other statements which had to be taken before I was ready for yours. Now, I promise you, you have all our attention. I have a few more questions to ask. In connection with the death of Michael Underhill.'

'Oh that.'

'Yes, that.'

'I'm not making any more statements without my solicitor being present.'

'That's rather a pity,' said the inspector. 'I had hoped that your help in the matter of the murder would outweigh your little escapade at the factory. But you don't seem to want it that way. You made a voluntary statement about that affair, and yet when I ask you about the murder you suddenly want your solicitor present. You surprise me, Mr Foulkes. You give me to wonder.' The inspector was speaking more in sorrow than in anger.

'But I don't know anything about the murder,' Eric explained carefully. 'I thought it was commonly supposed that Mary Jennings had killed him. They were lovers.'

141

The inspector nodded encouragingly. Let the man say anything at all and the rest would follow. 'Do you share that supposition?' he asked.

'I didn't say that. But I can't think of a better one.'

'When would you suppose that it happened?'

'I still want my solicitor,' Eric said.

'Then you shall have him. But there are some things we couldn't discuss at all in his presence. You're quite sure that you want him here now? Before you've heard my questions?'

Eric fell silent, staring at the table-top. What had the others said? And what were they going to say? He looked up at the policeman. 'Did you mean that if I helped you on the murder you'd forget about the other thing?' he asked.

'It's not for me to say. But I don't think you'd be prosecuted for the raid on the factory.' The constable, taking notes at a corner table behind Eric's shoulder, knew better than to record that truthful but highly improper remark.

'I'd heard that he grabbed her out of another man's car. The army officer. And that she stabbed him with his own knife when he got rough.'

'That would be on the morning prior to the raid on the factory,' the inspector pointed out. 'It would have happened in a city street. We know the place. There was no sign of blood there. But there were traces of mud and pine-needles along one side of his clothing and even in his hair. Do you really go along with that supposition?'

There was another silence. Then Eric sighed. 'No,' he said. 'I don't. Mrs Colcarth drove herself and Mary to the factory. Mike brought the rest of us in his car. He was alive when we left him. The Wendocks and that student and I went to the factory. Mary was to watch and see whether the two security men were both engrossed in getting the Daimler going again and then she was to catch us up and stand guard. Mike was to stay with the car and be ready to cause a diversion or come to our help if anything went wrong.'

'And did Mary catch you up?'

'Yes. We left her guarding our retreat. She was supposed to paint some slogans while we were inside. I suppose she was disturbed by whoever it was that trapped the rest of us, and ran for it.' Eric was speaking more easily now. 'My guess would be that the quarrel broke out again shortly after that.'

'Time?'

'Around one a.m.'

'That fits with the bracket which the pathologist gave us,' said the inspector. He gave Eric a congratulatory smile, almost a pat on the head for the bright boy of the class. 'Go on.'

'But that's all I know, Inspector.' Eric drew his feet back, ready to stand and leave.

'Nonsense,' said the inspector. 'I'm sure you know more than you think you do. What was talked about on your drive to the factory?'

'What we were going to do.'

'But between Mike Underhill and Terry Janson, for instance, what was said?'

Eric shrugged. 'Something seemed to be rankling between them, something they didn't want to discuss in front of the rest of us. They were sniping at each other with secret hints. You know what I mean?'

'I know exactly. Did you stop for petrol on the way to the factory?'

Eric stared at him. 'As a matter of fact, we did.'

'Who paid?'

'Really, Inspector—'

'It's important,' Cheyne said.

Eric thought as quickly as he could, through rising panic. Three other people, one of them still alive, had

143

been crammed into the car; and the pump attendant had been at the window. 'Mike didn't have enough on him. He borrowed from the rest of us.'

'We'll move on again,' the inspector said. 'Where did you leave the car?'

'There's a track further along the road.'

'So you walked back, on tarmac at first. And then went along the ditch?'

'Yes.'

'All together?'

Eric's skin crawled but it was too late to retreat. He fought to look and sound unconcerned despite his maddening catarrh. He wiped his nose and went on. 'We walked quietly along the road together, except that Mike stayed with the car. When we reached the culvert, we took to the ditch.'

'In what order?'

'No particular order, Inspector.'

'One of you must have gone first,' Cheyne pointed out.

'I don't remember.' Eric clamped his mouth shut.

Cheyne guessed that he had got all that was coming easily. 'Luckily, I can refresh your memory,' he said. 'It's been your week for leaving tracks around the countryside. But then, it's been good weather for tracks. It turned dry and then frosty after a wet period. We couldn't ask for better. The ditch was empty but with wet clay at the bottom, and your footprints were perfectly preserved. Hugh Wendock went first, didn't he? Then his wife, then Terry Janson and then yourself.'

'Perhaps,' Eric said huskily. 'I don't remember.'

'Do you remember why you were hurrying?' There was a moment of dead silence. 'The tracks show it clearly. The two Wendocks and young Janson moving slowly, almost on tiptoe, and then your tracks scuttling along behind, often overlapping the others. They read

144

like a book, Mr Foulkes. You were trying to move quickly but without making a sound.'

'I want my solicitor,' Eric said.

'Just one or two more questions,' said Cheyne. 'You know you don't have to answer them. Something happened between the other three during their walk up the ditch. If you were following on their heels you can tell me what it was.'

Eric made no answer.

'Why didn't you give Mike Underhill his share of the money you got for the mink?'

Eric shook his head.

'You told us that you hadn't received the money, despite the statement made by the dealer. But we found the whole sum tucked away behind the fuseboard in your bungalow. You'd been holding out on him, hadn't you? Was it because your debts were so pressing?'

Eric Foulkes put his head down into his hands.

'In fairness, let me tell you some more of what comes out of the pathologist's report,' Cheyne went on. He opened a folder. 'I'll just hit the high spots. The knife was forced between the ribs and twisted, with such force that one of the ribs was cracked and almost severed. The pathologist suggests that considerable strength would have been employed, more than that of a girl or even of an average man. Your hands and arms are highly developed. The knife missed the heart but severed a major artery. Fatal knife-wounds often don't bleed enough to soak the victim's clothing, Mr Foulkes, but in this instance, because of the twisting of the knife and the interval before the heart stopped, there was copious bleeding. The clothes which you were wearing that night showed spots of human blood. Not your own blood, Mr Foulkes, although it could be that of Mike Underhill. You're Group O and he was AB. Even your Rhesus factors are different.'

The inspector paused, but when Eric was silent he resumed. 'As I reconstruct the events, Mr Foulkes, you resolved to kill Mike Underhill so that you could keep the money for yourself. You set off with the others, but turned back—'

'No!' Eric said suddenly. 'I refuse even to listen to this nonsense. I insist on my solicitor being fetched.'

'All in good time,' the inspector said. 'Tell me, why did you decide to kill Terry Janson and Mrs Wendock?'

Eric went back to head-shaking, silent except for an almost inaudible whimper.

'When my men went to fetch you last night,' Cheyne went on, 'they served a search-warrant on you and then brought you here. Two men stayed to go through your house. They were thorough and they found the money you'd hidden. They thought that that was all and they were on the point of leaving when one of them decided to take a look at your garage. He was intrigued to find a heavy plank across the bottom of the garage door, wedged in place by shorter pieces of timber which were jammed against the corner of the back door on one side and the base of a tree on the other. He removed the shoring and opened the garage door. And what do you suppose he found?'

'What?' Eric asked through his fingers.

'He found Mrs Wendock and Terry Janson, as you very well know. There was still a high level of carbon monoxide in the garage, but an examination of Mrs Wendock's car was soon possible. The carburettor had been adjusted for very fast running, and there was a wire between the battery and the coil to ensure that once the engine was started the switch wouldn't stop it again.'

'I don't know anything about it,' Eric whispered.

'I'm afraid that you do. And your victims are convinced of it. They only survived because young

146

Janson had the quickness of mind to stall the car. The reason why we've had to keep you here in suspense for so long is that we were waiting for them to recover sufficiently to make statements, which they have now done.'

'They were trying to blackmail me,' Eric said. He sat up and blew his nose. From somewhere he found a trace of his dignity. 'Whatever else I may be, I didn't set out to kill. I needed all the money to save me from disaster, that's true. So I put off sharing it with . . . the others. You may as well know that Terry Janson was at the fur farm with us. I held that back,' he added bitterly, 'and look at the thanks I got. I was going to suggest we did another, similar job together to raise their shares. I had been avoiding Mike until I could find the right place. Mike was the one who cared about the money; Terry was only along for kicks.

'But Mike came after me. He caught up just as the others took to the ditch and flashed that knife at me. Hardly a word was spoken, and those were in whispers, but I knew that he was going over the edge. He was dangerous, waving that knife around. I grabbed his fist with the knife in it. And as you said, Inspector, my hands and arms are very strong. It's the work I do, you see. But I was only defending myself.'

'A court may believe that,' said Inspector Cheyne.

'We'd only come a short way,' Eric said. Now that he had started to talk he found that he could hardly stop. 'So I carried him back to his car. I put him down while I opened the boot. I caught up with the others as they reached the factory. I didn't think they realised that I wasn't on their heels all the way.'

'That seems quite clear,' said the inspector. He looked at the constable, who nodded. 'Now, while a statement is typed up for your signature – if you agree it, of course, only if you agree it – you'd better come and show us this track.'

'Very well,' Eric said. He was quite calm now. He even managed a crooked smile. 'But first, satisfy my curiosity. What did happen in the ditch which I should have known about?'

'Something very human,' said the inspector. 'For most of the way along the ditch, Hugh Wendock led the way followed by his wife, with Mr Janson third. Then it was clear from the tracks that Mrs Wendock jumped and turned round and after that Mr Janson was made to walk in front. It seems that he'd put his hand up Mrs Wendock's skirt. From something the lady said while making her statement, it was the coldness of his hand rather than its presence which she resented most. Now, shall we go?'

TWENTY

While he waited for the emotional storm to blow itself out, Jonathan tried to make sense of the puzzle. For the second time, she had thrown his ideas into confusion. And he had to believe her. There was no doubting the sincerity of her outburst.

She sat back at last, hugging herself. She was shivering now and Jonathan realised that she was at the very end of her tether. He would have taken the knife away from her except that, when it glinted suddenly in the dash-lights, he realised that she was holding it against her own throat – whether deliberately or because her arms were crossed over her breast he could not guess.

She began to speak in a hushed monotone, to nobody in particular. The effect was eerie and he felt the hair crawl on his neck. 'Nowhere to run,' she said. 'Nowhere to go. Wherever I turn, they're waiting. No Mike any more, he's gone for ever. He wasn't so much, but he never let anyone hurt me. Except himself and I didn't mind that.'

Jonathan wondered what to say and could think of nothing. Perhaps it was better for her to let it out.

'Now I've nobody and nothing. Let them all down. I let your sister down too. I promised I wouldn't let anyone else be hurt. Troubles ahead. I'll only make things worse by being around. Better if I'm not here.'

This train of thought should definitely be interrupted. Jonathan could only think of lighting two cigarettes and passing one to her. To his surprise, she accepted it with her unencumbered hand and took a deep pull, exhaling the smoke with a shuddering sigh. When she spoke again, she was at least speaking to him as a person.

149

'I'll only be making things worse for everybody,' she said. 'You do see that? The police are sure that I killed Mike. I shouldn't have run off. Flight's evidence of guilt, isn't it? On my own, I think I could stand up and face a murder trial and prison. But it would bring more disgrace on the others when they've got their own trials to face.

'All right, they're not the saints and martyrs I thought they were. I can see now that they've been doing it all the wrong way, but at least they've been trying hard to do some good, which is more than you can say about most of the rotten people in this rotten world. They're good people, better than I am. They deserve better than to have me around making bad worse.

'And there's my parents. They're respectable and proud of it. Me, on trial for killing my lover, would finish them. God, what it would do to them!'

'Hold on,' Jonathan said helplessly. 'These things do blow over.'

'A suicide blows over a damned sight quicker than a murder trial,' she retorted. 'You were right. There was no way I could hold a knife on both of you while I got the money out of him, and no way I could have got clear. I was just desperate, living in a dream-world. And now I'm not desperate any more and there are no more dreams.'

The new calm in her voice was more frightening than the earlier hysteria. 'You haven't thought it through,' Jonathan said.

'I've made up my mind. You stay here. I don't want to mess your nice car up.' She fumbled for the door-handle.

'You're acting on emotion,' Jonathan said urgently, 'not rational thought. Don't do anything you can't undo until we've talked it out. You could have a lot to live for.'

'Like what?' she asked. 'Go on, tell me the usual. Say I'm an attractive girl. That's the kind of thing they say, isn't it?'

Jonathan chose his words. 'At the moment, in those yachtsmen's castoffs, you're a mess,' he said firmly. 'When I first saw you, tarted up like a rock-group's camp-follower, I thought you ought to be drowned in a bucket. But when I found you beside my car, even though I was worried sick about Shona, I couldn't help thinking that a girl with your looks could do a hell of a lot better than Mike. Yes, you're attractive. You'll never be truly beautiful but, dressed right and properly made up, by God you could make men turn their heads!'

'You mean that?' she asked.

'You could turn my head any time.'

'Balls! You're just saying that.'

'That's what I thought when I started to say it,' he admitted. 'Now I'm as surprised as you are to find that it's true. So at least let's talk over your problems.'

'What good will that do?'

'What harm, except to buy you a few more minutes of life? We can see what the real issues are.'

'I know what they are. How does this damn thing open?'

'I'll open it for you,' Jonathan said, 'and I'll let you go off and do whatever you want, even though the idea tears me apart, if only you'll tell me what really happened and let's see if there isn't a better way. It'd be foolish to do something irreversible first. You can't change your mind afterwards. And I won't fancy you so much when you're dead.'

'Would you put flowers on my grave?'

'For a while, until I met somebody else.'

She stirred and his guts churned as he thought that she was making a move with the knife. He was half-

151

expecting the car to be sprayed with a fountain of her blood. But it was only a shrug.

'What difference can a little time make?' she said. 'I'm going to do it anyway. Remember, you promised.'

'I'll remember. What happened after I left you in the car?'

'It seems so long ago,' she said. 'I just sat, wondering what to do, wondering what I could say to the police to explain things away.

'Then, suddenly, Mike was at the door. He pulled me out and wanted to know what I'd said to you. I told him that, apart from warning you that your dog had been poisoned, I hadn't given anything away. I hadn't, had I?'

'Not a thing,' Jonathan said. There was no point in forcing more guilt onto her. 'You forgot to take the tongs.'

'There was too much emotion for thinking about practical things. I calmed him down. I usually managed to. Nothing and nobody else could,' she said with a hint of pathetic pride. 'I think I was good for him, in a way.

'He was having a few days' holiday which were due him, so he didn't have to go back to work. We went back to the flat so that I could change my clothes, your dog had been sick all over me, and we stayed there until it was time to go out again. We made love,' she remembered. 'It was as if we knew it was our last time. It was the best ever.'

'Did anyone see you? Coming or going, I mean.'

'I shouldn't think so. You mean, so that I could prove that he was still alive at that time? Mike drove us out to the factory. We picked up Eric and that student with the ears – neither of them has a car; and the Wendocks' Mini was too small to take us all. I switched into Mrs Colcarth's Daimler to make room. They all know that he was alive. But I can't ask them to say how they know, can I?'

'Time enough to think about proof when we know a little more,' Jonathan said. 'What happened at the factory? In as much detail as you can remember. I won't pass on anything you tell me.'

'This is a waste of time,' she said desolately, 'and I've so little time left. Put your arm round me. I want a cuddle before I go. Not if you don't want to,' she added.

'I want to.' He put his arm about her shoulders and she leaned against him, drawing comfort.

'Keep your hand away from the knife,' she said. 'I'll go on, shall I?

'Mike was to stay with his car while Eric and the Wendocks and Big Ears, whatever his name is, headed for the factory along a ditch they knew about. I got out before the factory and watched to make sure that Mrs Colcarth had both the security men involved with that big car of hers. Eric had shown her how to flood the engine, whatever that means.

'Then I took a bit of a short cut and caught up with the others near the corner of the factory. They were having a bit of a barney in some bushes.'

'What about?' Jonathan asked.

'I don't know. I asked Eric, but he didn't seem to know either. Anyway, we went over to the factory. They broke a window, using paper and some sticky stuff to avoid making a lot of noise, and went inside.

'My job was to stand guard and try to give them warning if anything went wrong. In case of trouble, or when they were finished, I was to get back to the road and signal to Mike with a torch and he'd come and pick them up or, if necessary, create a diversion or come to the rescue, whatever was needed. I'm making it all sound very complicated,' she added.

'It's quite clear. Go on.' Jonathan said. His arm was going to sleep, but the contact seemed to be soothing her so he decided to ignore the discomfort.

'Well, while I waited I was supposed to paint "Animal Murderers!", as big as I could, on the wall with an aerosol, so I had to move round the corner to the front. And before I could even get started, I saw a man's figure coming towards me and there was another one between me and the broken window. I didn't know what to do. What should I have done?'

'Run like hell,' Jonathan said.

'I'm glad you say so, because that's what I did. And I found that I could keep ahead easily. Those men couldn't run for toffee.' (Jonathan made a mental note, for CSM Heather's benefit.)

'I got back to the car and Mike wasn't there. I couldn't believe it. The men weren't very far behind. I knew that if they got Mike's car they could trace him, so it seemed better to take it away. I had a spare key in my pocket. Mike had given it to me so that I could get into the car any time I got back from shopping before he did. I'd hardly ever driven in my life, but it all seemed to happen for me. I even found the lights first time. The gears wouldn't seem to go right for me at first, but at least I was going faster than those men could run.

'I wasn't sure what Mike would expect me to do next. I thought I might do more harm than good if I went back. If Mike wasn't there he must have been at Mrs Colcarth's car, I thought, and they could all get away in that. But if I went back to the flat they could phone there if they still wanted me.

'It wasn't that easy. By about the time I was passing your barracks the excitement was over, and when I began to think about my driving I found that I couldn't manage. I'd been all right when I didn't think about it. And the town was coming up, with traffic-lights and roundabouts and pedestrian crossings and things, so I decided to give up, leave the car at the station and go the rest of the way by train. That maybe wasn't too clever,

154

but it was the best I could think of. And as it turned out, it didn't matter.

'I'd left a bag with some spare clothes in the boot, in case we got wet or something. It was when I went to get it out that I found . . . him.'

The car was getting cold. Jonathan started the engine. He lit two more cigarettes, one-handed. 'You should have called the police at once. Then they'd have had a much more accurate idea of the time of death, and they wouldn't have been confused by your absence.'

'I couldn't call the police just then,' she said. 'What could I have told them, while the others were probably still in the factory?'

'But this was far more serious than an Animal Rights prank.'

'I couldn't think it out at the time. I just knew that the police would visit the flat as soon as he was found. I walked around looking for somewhere to lose myself and I thought of the boats.'

A silence fell which Jonathan was almost afraid to break. At last he said, 'So somebody stabbed him, at or near the car, between the time you left him there and the time you were chased back again.'

'Obviously,' she said. 'And, during that time, the others were together and Mrs Colcarth was with the men at the gates. That only leaves me.'

Jonathan pushed aside the thought that it also left himself not far away and nursing not one but two thumping grudges. And his men, who had killed on his orders in the past. 'Who was it who diddled him of the money?' he asked.

'Eric.'

'Eric Foulkes? He's been charged in connection with the raid on the mink farm,' Jonathan said. 'I saw it in the Stop Press last night. So the police probably have the money.'

'That just makes it all the more hopeless,' she said dully. 'Eric was with the others and they left Mike alive.'

'You don't know that he stayed with the others,' he said.

'Yes I do. It's hopeless.' She fumbled again for the door-handle and this time found it. The interior light came on, seeming to blaze after the darkness.

The inrush of cold air cleared not only the tobacco smoke. It seemed to blow the fog out of Jonathan's mind. His arm was still round her. He tightened his grip and took hold of her wrist before she could more than stir. 'Wait,' he said.

The knife was in her other hand. 'Let go of me or I'll do it here.'

He held on. 'You don't have to do it at all,' he said. 'You're in the clear. Give me a moment to think.'

She almost slashed at him but she checked her hand. Jonathan thought frantically, fitting together his recollections of the radioed reports with what she had just told him. 'Eric killed your boyfriend,' he said.

'Why would he do that?'

'You just said it. He was holding out on Mike's money. And he wasn't with the others all the way or he would have known what they were arguing about. He could have stopped long enough to have a fight with Mike. Couldn't he?'

'I suppose so,' she said. 'But it doesn't help. How could we prove it?'

Another inspiration hit him. 'We may not have to. Why do you think the police were there, with lamps, where Mike's car had been standing?'

'Looking for evidence,' she said. 'Obviously.'

'But evidence of what? After catching your friends inside the factory, they wouldn't bother unduly, several days later, about where the car had been parked. Those floodlights indicated that they were doing a thorough search around what they knew to be a murder scene.'

She pulled against his hand, but not very hard. 'So what?' she said.

'If they'd found the place several days ago, they'd have finished up in daylight and been gone by now. They've turned out in the dark because they've got something new. And whatever it is, it can't do you anything but good. Somebody's started to talk. They may even have a confession.'

She let him lean across her to close the door and then she leaned again into the crook of his arm, but she held onto the knife.

'You're sure?' she asked.

He was far from sure. There were holes in his argument that he prayed she wouldn't see. For a start, one of the others might only now have confessed details of the raid, thereby also giving the police the clue to the murder site. But anything was better than letting this young person – this rather charming young person in her own way – slash her throat and end a life which could soon be full of promise again.

'I'm certain,' he said. 'You'll see.'

'They'll be angry with me for running off.'

'Not a bit of it. They'll be too glad to have found the missing witness.'

She said, in a very small voice, 'It's all going to be a bit heavy, isn't it? I don't know if I can cope. Suddenly, I don't have any friends any more.'

'You've got me,' he said.

'You promise again?'

'I promise again.'

She turned within the circle of his arm. He never decided who began the kiss, but it seemed to last until there was no emotion left to express. Then she released his arm and he backed the car out into the road.

She was silent while half a mile went by. As they passed Dr Whelks's house again, she whispered something. He thought that it was, 'Thank you.'

He pulled up near the floodlit track, took the knife from her limp fingers and dropped it under the seat. A policeman came to the window.

'Good evening, Officer,' Jonathan said. 'This young lady would like to make a statement.'